THE MUFFIN MAN

André Rostant

The Muffin Man
By André Rostant

ISBN: 978-1-912092-37-6

First published in 2024

Published by Palavro, an imprint of
the Arkbound Foundation (Publishers)

Arkbound is a social enterprise that aims to promote social inclusion, community development and artistic talent. It sponsors publications by disadvantaged authors and covers issues that engage wider social concerns. Arkbound fully embraces sustainability and environmental protection. It endeavours to use material that is renewable, recyclable or sourced from sustainable forest.

Arkbound
Rogart Street Campus
4 Rogart Street
Glasgow, G40 2AA

www.arkbound.com

www.carbonbalancedprint.com
CBP2278

THE MUFFIN MAN

André Rostant

palavro
PUBLISHING

SUPPORTERS

The publication of this book was enabled through a
dedicated crowdfunding campaign on Crowdbound.org.
Among the many supporters, we are particularly grateful to:-

Ellen Boulton

We searched for Troy but found Byzantium
Now we have seen it we will journey home

CONTENTS

FOREWORD

This is one of the strongest pieces of writing I have read in a very long time. André Rostant's sense of character and place is astonishing, and the picture he paints of life on the streets of modern London gives us a view of the town from the underside not matched since the time of Dickens or Henry Mayhew.

Rostant is a Londoner. The feelings of the people who inhabit his London are his feelings, not those of some outside observer. There is harshness here, and pain, but also humour and enormous humanity. And it is all viewed with such empathic accuracy that the reader needs no great leap of imagination to see her/himself in Rostant's world, where hope and despair are in constant conflict.

After reading this book, you'll never pass a homeless person or a Big Issue seller again without sympathy. You may even feel your own sense of humanity bolstered.

Anton Gill, August 2023

THE VENDOR

On the rain-glossed pavement, surrounded by scattered bones of dead umbrellas, the fringes of a black plastic bag of dogshit flutter. The wind that shakes the plastic begs a question of this bleak September afternoon: who scoops shit up in a bag to fling it down again?

Hapless deckhand struggling with a loose sail, a Big Issue vendor tacks his red Poundland brolly here and there against the tempest. The shower, momently turned to hail, gusts it inside out, then suddenly strips the fabric from the spokes altogether, whipping it away spinning like a dervish drunk on divinity. 'There goes your tarpaulin overboard!' a passer-by laughs.

I will call the vendor George. He is standing on Broadwick Street in Soho, outside Pret a Manger. George is from Kent, from Norfolk, from Scotland. In his late teens, he ran away to London to escape his abusive stepfather. George is from Halifax, from Devon, from Derbyshire. He joined the Army at eighteen. After six years of service, he left and drifted in and out of part time jobs until alcohol overwhelmed him. He defiled his youth as a rentboy in Soho, where he learned to speak Polari. She is a young woman who started taking crack and living in squats after running off to the Smoke from a foster home in Brighton at sixteen. He survived the wreck of the Essex by eating his dead crewmate.

George is, in fact, a 46-year-old from Romford. Pale, short, gaunt, balding. Homelessness followed in the wake of a messy divorce from a justly vindictive wife. His finances collapsed, he took even more to drink, and spending time on the street.

THE MUFFIN MAN

Now he lives between various central London hostels. He barely gets to see his seventeen-year-old daughter, never talks with his ex, and has not set eyes on his mother since his father died, twelve years ago.

In the dark rain is was yesterday, the shower passed, leaving George's magazines slightly damp at one end, but the pages not clumped, not especially tatty. He deemed them still saleable. A girl (he felt, at his age, he could reasonably call a young woman a girl), from one of the offices stopped by to give him a piece of cake. As she handed it him, smiling, he caught a hint of perfume.

George was absently mumbling to himself when a tall man in a cobalt-blue suit approached, engrossed in his own muttered soliloquy. George just about made out the words 'shitty' and 'fucking rag.' The suited man gave him a sideways scowl in passing. George idly wondered what this person with no dress sense was angry with. A crappy day at work? Not getting a leg-over last night? It could have been anything. The man had probably sworn at the woman on the ticket barrier that morning. He would surely descend to ratty nit-picking and quibbling later, unless hit by a bus on the way home. Vengeance is mine, sayeth his godlet, furiously blending the raisins of petty revenge in his divine pantry.

The Euphrates, we now learn, is a tributary of the Tyburn, which tree Howth himself missed, floundering in the Fleet, the stream of life, before working his charms on the King. It emanates from Eden all along to aqua the tame goose park, past Adam and Eve (of course), by way of the Lethe, broadening, deepening, branching into braided ekes round Thorney Island before it sinks down to a sunless Thames.

You can clearly see where the balloon of thought became untethered, where the dead dithered so the whole drunken ramble began to make sense.

But that was another time, another country. This Michaelmas afternoon, the elegant woman of perhaps forty, with her lustre of genteel Dublin condescension, slipped George a pound coin from a cheery smile. 'A contribution.' George proffered the magazine. His personal code was to offer whenever somebody dropped him money, whatever amount it might be. He would always fish out the correct change on a sale and ask, 'Are you sure?' if people refused. That way, he reasoned, he had kept some integrity. However many people did take their change or a magazine for one pound, George always finished the day up. He wondered why people so often call it a contribution. Contribution to what? He contemptuously threw the umbrella skeleton to the ground.

A small brownish scabby dog padded past, away around the corner. Then Lennie and another lean man, both beggars, came along. Lennie, a freckled, red-headed Cockney with a goatee. His gait, in essence, that of a satyr, from throwing himself under a tube train. He tottered on what looked like back-to-front legs; a springing motion. His companion, by some unknown injury or malady, was wont to swing his legs wide from the hip, throwing them forward as though wading through floods. The effect was a balletic harmony of movement between the two. 'Which way did Daisy go George? Which way did she go?' Lennie asked.

The vendor nodded toward the corner and the beggars waltzed off, after the dog, no more missed than leaves that fall slightly early, when one leaf clings on - a leg lost to the needle, another to a train, the neck or wrist braids of failure. More still think 'let them' than Dickens might have hoped of the 21st Century.

A man loomed, maybe in his thirties, French accent. 'The system... So unfair. I am going to buy a tent, you know. A tent... You got to survive. You can't get away from the system, non. People 'ave the system in their heads, you know, in their brains.' George asked where this fellow intended to camp once he got his tent. 'You've got to hide... I just survive.' The man was dressed warmly, if scruffily, carrying a small, crocheted clown under his arm. He turned, drifted away to reveal another figure in a duffel coat and corduroy pants who, for a moment, George thought was spray-painting the little bag of dogshit orange. But no. This other man was marking florescent exes on Westminster's broken paving stones, photographing them, registering them on a hand-held gadget. Without being asked, he looked up explaining that, before, the Council would repair the pavement then charge it to various utility companies whose plant it covered. But of late, the gas, electric, and other firms paid the contractors themselves direct. This clarified nothing. Susan's virginal cog.

Low on magazines, George... Let's make this narrative simpler. George can speak for himself. Let us look out through his mistaken, bloodshot eyes, and share his incomprehension of the world.

My notes are in diary form. They cannot all be transcribed coherently. In the writing, I have worked hard not to stray from the truth of what happened, as I remember it.

Low on magazines, I left this pitch to make the fifteen-minute walk to Long Acre in Covent Garden to buy more from the barrow there. Oxford Circus would have been closer, but I found the bloke on that barrow such a miserable old sod. As I passed through Leicester Square, I gave a nod to the one-legged Buddhist monk, with his smooth-as-an-egg head, draped in his burgundy and saffron robes. Our smiling, chubby brother's main activity was handing people plastic gold charms, paper prayers, then asking for donations.

Do not imagine for one moment that reality will dominate this tale, this journey. The West End you know will melt away like time itself; day from night will fall confused before the twilight of its end. You will encounter faerie folk. This is a fairy story.

Or passing, or to come

Next morning, in Soho, a white, presumably English, woman asked, 'Where are you from?' I said Romford, she replied, 'Good. It's just that some of these eastern European fellows… I can't believe they don't have an actual home back in Poland.' She gave me a pound. I made no comment. My hair is thick, curly, chestnut brown. I am quite tall, with a tan. My father hailed from Wicklow in Ireland, a tinsmith. My mother was of Italian parents, raised in Wicklow. I hate them, her more than him, with every fibre of my being.

I have found happiness in the Way of the Red Tabard. Not that I do not have my demons. I saw them; I still do. They crowd me sometimes. Sometimes they talk to me. I followed one, a fluffy black lamb, down Old Compton Street on a Wednesday in that year… It was weak. One of its eyes had been put out, leaving a bloody wound. The other eye was sewn shut. Eventually, it wandered into a shop. I didn't dare follow it.

THE MUFFIN MAN

When I first set out to write, it was because it struck me that politicians, academics, the press, they all have, everybody has, opinions on who we are, what we are. Often they have fucking horrible opinions. Many people who stop to talk with a vendor want to know, 'What's your story?' They can ask us because we are homeless. When last did you ask your dentist or the supermarket till worker, 'What's your story, then? How did you come to be doing this?' Most do not really want to know our story. At least, they do not appear to. They only want to properly satisfy themselves that we vendors have some defect, so real folk may rest assured we are a distinct case, species even. More still, crave confession and absolution. People are afraid of us. We crowd the fringes of their world along with past misdeeds, regrets. Fleeing souls floating toward them o'er the sea, debt, the government, more debt. But I am ahead of myself.

Then, it occurred to me that no matter what I write, no matter what Promethean feat any vendor achieves, no matter how sparkling their notions, how eloquent their elaboration of the vicissitudes of vendordom, they will still only ever fuel that narrative of redemption which is The Big Issue, and further burnish the brazen form of a tarnished sinner re-cast in bronze: the immutable icon of the cured leper.

We are a legion renowned for taking in those whose pasts and presents are best forgot, because ruinous. That is the rule. There be exceptions; they prove the rule. We are a red-tabarded order, an adoptive clan with all the solidarity of a league of cats. We are heroic; we render ourselves to catharsis. We stand, stigmatic milestones on the richest streets of London, measuring the space between shopping and reality, the distance twixt wealth and heaven. So long as those realms remain separate, we cannot rest. We haunt. Run a length of string to encompass Covent Garden, Soho, and environs. From Bond Street along Oxford Street to Holborn; down Kingsway to the River; on, up Northumberland Avenue, The Mall to St James Palace, back up Bond Street to Oxford Street.

This is the great eruv hazerot in which our tribe lives so much of its private business in public, where Shabbat is forever suspended so we may be endlessly cleansed of our iniquities through labour. *Yet, does that matter enough to warrant all this melodrama?* You could tackle the grotesque mundanity of it all head on, but that would be journalism, the medium of a moment that speaks to its own time and does our thinking for us. This urgency is a never-ending squirm; restless, glimmering riverbank mud flickering under the shadows of dragonfly wings at sunset, while Charon watches… waits. Besides, there is no narrative arc that could bind the ends of an overflow of hours flooding into weeks, into years, so that no story is tellable here. We reach a compromise. For themselves, episodes will build, collapse, recombine into something quite different from the sum of their parts.

Yesterday once more

Another rainy session outside Pret with no umbrella, no prospect of rescue by the coastguard nor any chance at building an ark. But I was finished quickly, toward the end of lunchtime. A Maghrebi convert earnestly impressed upon me the importance of testifying Christ's love for me: I should 'check out a born-again church,' rather than a Catholic one.

THE MUFFIN MAN

In fact, further up that week, too, a stranger prayed over me fervently, spreading a cold spidery hand on the crown of my bald, slightly bowed head. A woman bought me coffee early, for which I was grateful.

Sometimes I would buy my own coffee in the red round fish-eyed morning, usually from the Algerian Coffee Shop on Old Compton Street. Sometimes I would stand on a pitch all day, and nobody might think to ask nor buy me one. Not that anybody is obliged. While at other times, people spilled out of sandwich shops in crowds, bearing unsolicited beverage and food. I never asked, seldom refused. The bladder having a limited capacity, I came to an arrangement with loitering between-job couriers and builders on the site over the road, which kicked into operation once the kind coffee buyer had moved on (so as not to offend). Why do people not ask first? When I had not eaten by three, sometimes even if I had, I would buy chips at the Golden Union, where I once unexpectedly encountered the Wanker.

The afternoon dragged. An elegant one, another ostensibly Irish woman in, say, her late fifties, gave me £2. When I said she was kind, she replied that she was just 'trying to do justice.' Tom Baker, the best Doctor ever, nibbled a sandwich in Pret and gave me a pound on the way out, a proper gent. I told him to 'break a leg!' He smiled with all those teeth. He was probably doing a voiceover. There are lots of voiceover studios in Soho.

It mattered how I spoke, what I wore. I was too posh, too tidy, too sober, 'too intelligent' to be a vendor. People said outright: 'You don't have much of an accent.' I told them I went to grammar school. Then I remembered primary school, the funeral of the registers. Every morning and afternoon, solemn children in pairs, each holding one end of a pastel green laminated book in a procession of little biers, from and to the office.

Another yesterday

One morning I bumped into Martin, the Irish spot-beggar. That is, he goes around asking for money rather than sitting in one place. 'Morn. How're ye?"Ah, sure, grand tanks.'

Martin had gotten a flat some weeks earlier, via his key worker, street teams, and the council. A bedsit in Stockwell. Formerly a builder, labourer, plasterer-type person, living between Park Royal and Kilburn, he wanted to go back to work as a window cleaner once he was, as he put it, 'settled.' Martin was a mild, ghostly man, with a gentle Kerry accent and a lisp. His voice lilted soft; his conversation was vague yet measured. He had doe eyes. Though his face was wrinkled from drink and sleeping rough, it retained a calming smoothness. Even the callouses on his hands were like cushions. He faintly radiated an aura of uncertain serenity.

Martin bore a blanket over his shoulder or under his arm. He could not beg without it.

He told me he would watch soaps in the flat. I did not hear him call himself an alcoholic. He was always cogent, articulate, and alert when we talked. He reported downing half a bottle of whiskey in one as having warmed him up a bit for the morning.

He felt too 'prescribed' in the flat, too restricted, too claustrophobic. It drove him mad sometimes to be confined there. The location made it difficult for him to go begging. I know Stockwell. A soft-spoken mild-mannered beggar like Martin would struggle there. In the West End, he patrolled regular routes, had regular customers. His description of givers being customers strikes me as wholly appropriate. People who give (correct me if I am mistaken) appear to gain a degree of gratification, so Martin could be described as having been of service. But that is just my opinion.

Martin spent a great deal of time sleeping rough. He continued to sleep out even after he got the flat, especially in mild weather. If he was out begging, he might bed down where he stopped, or wanted, to start back in the morning. He was especially fond of sleeping in Covent Garden Piazza, North arcade. 'I'll keep on hamaneggin it for an hour or two now, until I've enough for me tea ... Yes...' 'He continued, following his own counsel, 'I'll go down to...' His destination receded in a mist of musings. Martin smiled enigmatically and ambled away after it, half turning to wave before he faded.

Look, I understand, we are all trying to get in. But if you keep pushing and shoving, we won't all fit through that little gate at once now, will we?

Days ago

My phone buzzed, the following morning. A text from Melanie, my daughter: *Gran dead. Funeral tomorrow. Soz.* It must have been sudden. I was not going to call Melanie. I certainly wasn't going to any funeral. Good riddance!

THE MAN WITH THE STICK

I had arrived outside Pret, the morning of Martinmas Eve. The warm aroma of croissant and coffee making me dreamy, I spotted Scottish Todd. Crotchety fellow with a frightful temper, my age. Used to be a rentboy. He beckoned feebly, his back to the John Snow, braced against the pub, left arm splayed, simultaneously leaning on his stick with the right hand. He quailed lest he should tumble into infinity were he to move from the wall. A lost child with his lollipop round head and cropped dun-coloured, thinning hair. I helped him manoeuvre across Soho to a different pub. He abhorred the John Snow and was barred from most of the others. This was after ten. At every moment during the unbearable sloth of our consequent pained twenty-minute shuffle, my mind dwelled on the sales I must surely be missing and the heady croissant haze.

We hooked arms. You could see Todd had been a pretty youth, but time, stress, poverty, drink, and debauchery had taken their toll, so life now found him spotty and scabby. Some of his spots oozed pus; some of the scabs wept. He would nearly always be in the same leather bomber jacket and jeans, both worn: a tattered coat upon a stick before his time. Todd had a runny nose, which he kept pausing to wipe with the palm and heel of the hand that held my sleeve. Unable to walk more than fifty metres unaided, even with his stick, he lived in constant dread of being found fit for work by benefit assessors. As we hobbled along, he talked at length of his flatmate and drinking companion, Bill, a big alcoholic

THE MUFFIN MAN

Cornishman. Bill suffered from diabetes and was, at present, in hospital, having a toe amputated. When I say flatmate, Bill rented from a housing Co-op and Todd crashed, buckshee.

Todd had spent the night drinking vermouth in Old Compton Street. He was even more unsteady than usual. Now he clung tight to my naked arm—my sleeve ridden up—with his nose-wiping hand, sweating like a bitch, boils and scabs all the while disgorging. He became agitated, swore loudly and fiercely at everyone and everything that threatened to slow our funereal progress. He reeled exaggeratedly at the tiniest, remotest threat of obstruction, mobile or static.

As we inched awkwardly past G-A-Y, where he often drank, Todd fumed about what hypocrites former rentboys were. Many now married, with a child or two, and denied their pasts. He confided that he was still considered quite a catch by some girls in his small hometown near Dundee, being the last bachelor there bearing his clan's name. Not because he is a Greek god. He intimated that living in London, albeit it gave him an allure, had broadened his outlook too much to take up with an orange, stilted hometown girl. Dance nimbly o'er the sun-bright rocks and streams.

He spoke wistfully of his years on the game, not saying it outright, but sidling toward the suggestion that he had been more of a courtesan to rich gay men in the sense of sparkling company than by way of carnal prostitution. He lamented piles of money made and thrown away, much of it on those same people who now want to forget him or muddy their shared past, who condemn him for letting himself go, for letting rich potential partners or sugar daddies get away, for drinking in low-life company. My thoughts all croissants and missed sales, I barely heeded his cackling. Bed softly on a moon-bathed moss of dreams.

On parting, he rewarded my sacrifice with a contemptuously delivered coup de grâce: 'Tae think I've come tae this: half crippled, bein helped doon the road be a Big Issue seller!' I smiled as gently as I was able, internally screaming, wishing I could burn the sleeve of my coat or bleach my arm. It took five minutes to regain my pitch, and twenty more to rationalise the episode to the point where I could see its humour and my own hypocrisy. I did not know ... I cannot remember ... No, what? Wait. It doesn't matter.

The Curse

I was looking forward to a rainy afternoon, equipped with a dainty, black-frilled umbrella, perfectly suited to a New Orleans funeral. A half-full bottle of energy drink lay in the gutter. Bees crawled in and out, fussing around it. They had been nesting there for weeks. I was agitated by my tortured expedition with Todd. Lennie and Dan (I had learned the other beggar's name) pirouetted, stalled, perned, and gyrated away toward Ingestre Place in search of a dealer. Daisy padded after them. They were a short way past me when Lennie bumped into a woman. She let out a shriek. She wore a neat flower print blouse and well-tailored blue trouser suit. She was tall, appeared to be in her early twenties, with black shoulder-length ringlets and a heavy fringe. Fair to the extent that she might possibly be made of porcelain. A confident stunner, in the company of an even taller, smartly suited man who stopped and turned. 'Fuck's sake!' he barked at Lennie.

THE MUFFIN MAN

The woman, embarrassed, pulled at his arm. 'David, leave it, we're late.'

'No, Linda. These people are scum,' David snarled. 'Watch where you're fucking going, you crippled piece of shit! You mong!'

Lennie hobbled off, mumbling apologies. But I saw that, under his breath, he cursed them.

The Murder

Possibly in connection with drug dealing, there had been a fatal stabbing in Ingestre Place the August before. A local beggar. There were many theories and rumours. If Tolkien can pepper his work with random long-ass poems and nobody objects, so can I. Dolly the Hat's version be what you're getting. She had a mesmerising, gruff voice, a rasping whisper with nutty, mellow undertones. The combination made her storytelling that bit more atmospheric. Dolly's rind was mainly coarse, tobacco-yellow at the temples, neck and chins, redwood on the facial protuberances and lower arms, and charcoal grey toward the fingertips of her purple hands. She had gone straight to decomposing without taking the trouble to die. She had John the Baptist hair and tiny, crazy eyes, like currants embedded in scoops of Stilton. A gigantic woman with the mien of an aristocrat, she sported a splendid moustache. Dolly retained all her teeth, uniformly light brown, caked in plaque. She talked *to*, limiting any responses largely to that species of benign, patronising smirk which is so often misconstrued as a sign of enlightenment. She usually wore a Trilby. There were patches of fungus on her face, neck, and arms. I would not hazard a guess at her age; she could have been forty or a thousand and forty.

This is how Dolly recounted, while we shared a drink behind St Paul's, off the Piazza, cider dribbling from her chin, what she thought happened in Ingestre Place: 'You want to know what really befell Jolly John, lads? You know he got filleted, by Jove, that he did, up in Soho, the miserable shit. Whatever they say, I know what really happened and I believe Laura when she says she never did it.'

We settled down, and Dolly proceeded to chant her poem.

'Bright under the sun, this little street, this alleyway,
in stillness until a hurried man, almost out of breath
limps to a wall and halts.
Anxiously he glances back.
Bending, hands on his knees, he pants.
Fear presses hard on his heels.
About, beyond, Soho is all abuzz.
When is it not?

Ingestre Place is just out of the way enough
for the current of the crowd to flow past, unheeding.
He is wearing far too many clothes for this weather
and torrents of sweat sweep down his face, in a filthy flood.
Gurgled, laboured gasps vie with a wheezy cough
that judders round his wine-dark jowls,
flecked with the foam of his spit.
The man is a Big Issue vendor, under one arm,
suffering magazines, all damp, some torn.

THE MUFFIN MAN

Chasing his own shadow down the day,
a young man speeds as only a drug addict could race
in the hunt for hits, so quickly spots his prey
collapsing against the wall.
Flashing a blade, he pauses now.
He is near breathless himself.

He takes a moment to collect his wits
and when he's done, grins through decaying teeth at the frail
tramp,
slumped in a silent heap as if he was meditating there.
Knowing well the vendor will have cash, while he has none,
he looks to check if anybody's chanced upon them.

The two men are alone.
The hunter ventures to speak:
'Just give me what you've got, you Pikey cunt,
you silly old bastard.'
He grips his steely glistening knife tight.
His voice is shrill.
Briefly he falters, then holds forth anew:
'What's the fucking matter with you?
Do you speak English at all?'

There on the pavement, back to the bricks,
his victim sits gazing up at the glittering blade.
He appears transfixed.
One of his eyes is rotten: marbled, festering, dead.
Tutting, the mugger tries again.
The sound is harsh, his words snide:

'Fresh off the boat, are you? You stupid twat.
You're gonna learn.
I used to sell that load of bollocks.
Oh yeah, I did ... Working not begging,
don't make me laugh.
You're taking the piss. Fat, filthy old prick!
Sat there like a heap of shite.'

The vagrant waits without moving.
A dark stain where all is sun.
No other sound disturbs. A seagull cries, high above them.
'Stealing, not working!' The would-be hard-man sneers.
This is nothing to a war-toughened wanderer
who has coolly faced far finer foils
in much harsher worlds.

Suddenly the still one slumps, barely keeping his balance.
Then, with a grumbling, heaving groan he appears to
get larger:
his hands, his face, swell to a monstrous size.
His hair turns black while, all at once,
he starts to sprout a hideous beak!
This blade that was given to Johnny by a mate,
burns in his hand.
The youth jabs at the apparition.
He jabs in vain.

It is not a good sword. It is not a sword at all!
No fine wrought edge, no knotted hilt.
It is a piece of cheap crap from some industrial estate

THE MUFFIN MAN

in Wales or Chandigarh, and it snaps
like the feeblest toothpick the moment it touches the vendor.
Despite bright sunshine, in this spot the street grows dim.
The giant, hazy spectre lurches forward with a deep, breathy coo.
There, left after it, the shape of the man remains, hollow to see.
An eggshell-thin veneer on a ghostly void.

The huge, heavy pigeon falls grim upon the boy.
It has him fast, breathing its stinking breath over his face
turning its head to one side and glowering,
hot as Hellfire and reeking rank.
The creature's filthy frothing maw gapes.
It grunts and coos,
streams of tears springing from its jet-starred eyes;
one of them mottled and spoiled.
Johnny tries to push it off, it is too strong.
Such a weight!
Attempts to scream; nothing! Nothing!
Choking and whimpered gasps.

Somewhere sounds industrial clanking:
busy builders of never-finished London labour on.
Now it sets one claw upon his chest, one on his face.
It presses the boy's eye in gradually,
soon enough drawing blood then, in one rapid movement,
it punctures his neck fatally, with a great peck.
Relentlessly it treads the hapless fool on the ground,
writhing and crushing, its iridescent throat flickering
lilac, green, the down of its breast rough and damp
against the torn, bloodied corpse. It nudges and snorts,

shifting its shoulders' wild bulky brawn and hunches,
open-beaked, flapping its wings over the carcass.

Behind, the empty form of the man stirs to its feet.
Without the substance to support clothes,
it stands all the same.
The clothes stand with it, the whole thing
blindly feeling its way toward the flapping horror,
clambering onto its tail.
Once it has reached the back, it nestles in the feathers,
buries itself, so it begins to blend into the pigeon.
Soon you might only make out the red of the tabard:
THE BIG ISSUE OFFICIAL VENDOR,
the legend continues,
WHEN YOU BUY THE MAGAZINE PLEASE TAKE IT!
As though here struts a vendor-beast.
Yet the words, too, fade away, leaving nothing
but this coo-cooing freak, a giant Soho pigeon!

As this happens, Laura, the youth's girlfriend, runs up.
Not since the shadow of cholera darkened Broad Street
has such a frantic frenzied shrieking erupted here.
The clucking was enough, the going without a fix,
and now before her eyes there is a... pigeon
bigger than a man, risen on horrid, diseased feet.
It launches into the sky, up and away
from Laura's blood-soaked mate, with no great haste.
It ignores her fuss and flaps out of view,
over the Brewer Street rooves.

All screams and curses, she kneels by her boyfriend;
by what is left. She tries to cover his neck
and eye to stem the bleeding, but that is just hopeless.
She clasps her hands to her face, wailing and keening.
Staring round, she spots the hilt of the knife and takes it up
and wonders what it means.
She notices a cigarette butt lying next to her.
Without thought, she picks the fag up too and pockets it
in the breast of her denim jacket, with her other stuff,
all the while wildly shouting, 'Please, somebody fucking help!'
A crowd congregates, but nobody gets too close
until swarms of police descend en masse;
determined dolts.

And of course, they arrest her straight away.
'There was a pigeon. Did no-one see it?' she gibbers.
'There was a pigeon. Yes, love, yes there was,' the sergeant
answers.
'There really was a pigeon; I saw it with my own eyes.'
They lead her to an ambulance, drenched in her dead
boyfriend's life.
'See how they screw themselves up with their drugs,' the
sergeant says.
'A bloody mess.' The constable agrees.

PROSTITUTE SLAYS HEROIN ADDICT
was the line the papers followed on this one:
KILLED IN BROAD DAYLIGHT.
Every redtop screamed it louder than the widowed girl,
for the boy who shared her doorways,

stilled her arm for the needle, trudged with her
in the small hours through the rain to the dealer
and put his sour tongue to her rotten teeth.
Barely beyond their teens, in London,
out on the street.
Blue and white tape bobbed with the breeze in afternoon sun.
Police in forensic overalls busied themselves,
while the bovine gawking tourists and office workers gazed.
Over the road by the sandwich shop
an old man stooped, cradling his Big Issues,
distractedly.'

Dolly, triumphant, surveyed her spellbound audience. 'T'was the silent hopelessness in his heart that drew the Sluagh to him, boys.' She sighed.

Then up and spake a tall young Mancunian beggar, sat at Dolly's right knee: 'She's fucking lucky they don't still hang people. Fucking Old Bill!' The beggar had longish, scraggy black but slightly greying hair. He was skinny, with disparate teeth, looking fifty but I knew him to be thirty. He became a familiar acquaintance. Without pausing for breath, he talked on, complaining to the company that all morning he had been moved on by the police. He was not long after being arrested for begging and fined £180. Now he had been advised he would get an ASBO and could face up to a month in gaol, for persistent begging or not paying fines. He railed, calm and eloquent, with surprisingly little swearing, yet definitely railed, bemoaning the impossibility of paying the fine. He said, 'If you're a white English bloke with no particular alcohol or drug problem, you go to the bottom of the list. What fucking sense does it make to fine me £180? I don't claim any benefits at all. What fucking sense does it make to put me in jail, for £2000 a week? What fucking sense does it make that I could do more time in prison than a mugger or violent criminal? I could spend half my life in prison JUST FOR BEGGING!'

The Survivor

Names of months and dates no longer matter. You work in the factory, in the office, on the street, and as no two days are the same, no Mobius Tellurian gyre is any different from any other that fold back on itself or twist to bring up before us the face and voice of Craig. Craig, a vendor, originally from Stoke, not working now, he grumbled, riddled with arthritis.

While bottles and tins continued to circulate, Craig recounted the story of a cold, wet, winter's night. He addressed this forum of peers, elephant grey, his shoulders hunched in pain. He spoke breathlessly, with the slow, deliberate movements of somebody for whom even the shallow breathing he ventured brought suffering. His buckled silver face, cratered as the gibbous waning moon above, recalled — his lips following along with the words — the temperature was below zero as he waited for an outreach team from a hostel at Euston which, for whatever reason, never came. He gave out most of the last of his money hanging out in a King's Cross cafe, where he sat for some time, with the small of his back exposed to an icy draft from the door, too tired to notice, comfort eating. It was late, all that remained to eat were beautiful big, glazed cakes and cream puffs. Then, he said, he caught the tube to the shelter at Aldgate, to be told by those waiting that it would not open until six. When he eventually got in, he spent the morning shivering uncontrollably. Craig paused and looked around for approval. Unable to pierce our shield of bored silence, he ventured a second sweep of our faces but gave up and renewed his lament.

Craig told us he had joined the Paras at 17, from the cadets, spending the next 17 years in service. Left, he did, because, as he framed it, 'I couldn't face putting any more bullets through me mates' heads.' Apparently, with no prospect of medical evacuation and comrades' wounds being so severe, this man avers he finished them off like Grand National fallers rather than see them suffer. Years that no one talked of; times of horrid doubt, or filled with faith and hope and whacking and despair? I have no opinion about whether this is true. Someone coughed into the surrounding indifference. It is what he said. In any event, Craig told us he sold The Big Issue for a while in front of the barracks in Aldershot where, he recalled, former comrades, when they first encountered him, asked what he was doing 'begging'.' He took enormous offence, pointing out that selling The Big Issue is a business.

Craig summed up with, 'Everything is shit. I feel like shit!' Recognising at last, in this curt, bleak peroration, one truth capable of acknowledgment, all empathised, with general grunts. I put my arm round his shoulder and intoned words to the effect that we're all fucked, in various ways, and I wished I could do something more than empathise, to which he replied, 'You could give us a kiss.' And turned his cheek to me, which I duly pecked, remarking our stubbly chins might achieve a great Velcro effect. He departed, cheered by the company.

I have to say it: I cannot let it lie. This ex-Para vendor

THE MUFFIN MAN

Military Man man brings us to a curiosity: the SAS must be, or once have been, the biggest regiment—even if it is not a proper regiment—of a standing army larger than North Korea's. There is such a number of blokes (this is chiefly a male delusion) who falsely claim to have been in the Army, a great many of whom say, or imply, that they served in the SAS. Since we have the red outfits already, perhaps one year we could troop the colour instead of Household Division. We could use one of our own queens.

Politicians soft boil their wars, then dip soldiers in them. That is the way things have always been.

I recall another vendor who likely pretended to have served in the Army. He wore fatigues and walked with crutches. Though he claimed to have had all or most of his toes amputated, he sported fiercely bulled British Army boots, possibly the most uncomfortable footwear ever inflicted upon humankind. He was the Sergeant Whatsisname, who made riflemen from mud, who 'drilled a black man white' and made a mummy fight.

Now, I have no way of caring whether he was ever in any army, but this other vendor I knew to have really spent 21 years with the Royal Artillery found it puzzling, to the point of being incredible, that this man would reveal neither his Army number nor regiment, either of which would easily have verified his claims. This, to me, is a sensitive conundrum. It is perfectly possible the fellow was earnest, and equally possible he had genuinely come to believe his own delusion. We might, perhaps, have tested him by getting him to sing England's Soldiers of the Queen, to see if he could bring the same pathos to it as Edward Woodward.

There is a chance he was in the Army but felt the nature of his service not spicy or exciting enough. Whatever his reasons or authenticity, he pretended to be a soldier—a claim widely met with scepticism. He was described to me as a 'piss-taking cunt!' Which is sad, because everybody knows there are too many ex-service personnel on the street, along and overlapping with this vast cohort of fantasists who fought for that same England which, after all these years of still not caring, perhaps continues to dream of an Empire stretching from Strand to Holborn Hill. Perhaps he had seen the walls of Troy. At least he didn't claim to only have one leg.

And here, a confession. I am an addict. A Cheese addict. Stilton, to be precise. When I cannot get Stilton, I will devour any cheese. It is no substitute. I do not readily believe that any man having once tasted the divine luxuries of proper Stilton will afterwards descend to the gross mortal enjoyments of alcohol, heroin, or crack. Like de Quincey, I take it for granted that those will eat now who never ate before. And those who always ate, will eat the more.

GEORGE MICHAEL IS STILL ALIVE

Suki slinked gracefully from under the duvet, slipped lithely off the bed and glided out of the room, headed for the kitchen. Salvatori yawned and stretched. Niki reached over, stroking his cheek lazily, then she rolled onto her back and helped him climb up on her, in one smooth movement. 'Got you to myself, at last!' She could hear Suki in the kitchen. Salvatori nuzzled into her neck, but a loud meow distracted him. He looked up. With a shrug, he was off. He sprang from the bed, landing gracefully on all four paws, and padded to the kitchen where Suki was still mewing loudly. 'You fickle feline!'

After feeding the cats, Niki let them out into the garden. Mainly because she could not bear the thought of anything happening to them, and partly for the pragmatic reason that pure Siamese cats are expensive to replace. Niki had had the first ten metres of her garden caged with light mesh. The cats got the best of both worlds, with added security. You could not be too careful in Croydon lately; terrible things were happening to cats, with depressing regularity.

It was ten when Niki left the house. She took the tram to the station, and a train up to Waterloo. Rain teemed endlessly out of the September sky. From Waterloo, Niki walked over the Jubilee footbridge and through Charing Cross station where, on the forecourt, next to the Eleanor Cross, a small gaggle of people waited. It must be said, they seemed predominantly elderly.

'Good afternoon, er, Nicola?'

'Yes, that's me.'

'Chaz. Pleased to meet you.' The guide extended his hand.

He was a Londoner with a pleasant smile, wearing a cor blimey cap and scarf.

Niki was researching her latest novel, 'Sick as a Parrot', fourth in her highly successful Ravensbourne series. Stories featuring Lilith Ravensbourne, leading ornithologist, bird behavioural expert, and amateur sleuth. The first novel, 'The Three Feathers', saw Ravensbourne drawn into investigating the death of a Cambridgeshire ostrich farmer, on the face of it, trampled by his flock. The second book, 'Catch the Pigeon', involved drug smugglers using messenger pigeons to evade surveillance, and the third, 'The Angry Eagle', centred on the unexplained death of a Colonel in the Dutch army while training eagles to intercept drones. 'Sick as a Parrot' would diverge somewhat from the formula in that it concerned an unexplained disappearance and murder involving a masonic lodge whose emblem and banner featured two popinjays. As part of the historical background, Niki wanted to learn more about the Soho cholera outbreak of 1854, a central feature of Chaz's tour.

She was not keen on talking with the rest of the group, so, after Chaz wrapped up—explaining that Snow's removal of the Broad Street pump handle was merely a theatrical flourish—the Cholera was already abating, Niki declined an invitation to have a drink in the eponymous John Snow pub. Instead, she snatched a quick coffee in Pret. Upon leaving, she noticed a Big Issue vendor. Fishing in her purse, she could only find £2, so she handed it to him and said he should keep the magazine.

'That's kind of you.'

'I'm just trying to do justice.' She meant it. Who knows what might happen? Anybody could end up homeless.

On the train home, Niki sorted through her notes. She wanted to get straight down to writing while it was all still fresh in her mind.

Chaz was not having a good afternoon. The group dispersed; not one had left a tip. True, he had been paid, but you cannot live on the money from such a job. It relies on tips. Everybody in London has three jobs and none of us has any money. Since it was often the case with midweek pensioner-heavy tours that few tipped, Chaz was resigned to it. His actual problem this afternoon was fiddlier.

After the tour, he joined some of the pensioners for a swift half, but left hastily, not being much of a drinker and not really appreciating being pumped for more and more tour long after he was supposedly finished. He visited a shop on Carnaby Street and was returning past Pret when a bicycle courier whizzed past at breakneck speed on the pavement, clipping a dawdling pigeon.

The courier disappeared, leaving the bird with one wing crushed and its head knocked so hard an eye was now hanging out. There was nobody else in the street. Chaz might have walked away, but he could not leave the poor animal suffering. 'Come on, mate. I'll help you.' He said. On closer inspection, he realised there was nothing he could do to help the bird, it was too badly injured. 'I'm sorry, but there's nothing else for it.' He sighed. Reaching down, he attempted to pick up the pigeon, to wring its neck, although he had never done such a thing. He lifted the bird gingerly, taking it with both hands, but it started, scaring him, so he let go.

Inside Pret, a couple of Indian tourists sat at the window seats with their seven-year-old son.

'Mummy, what's that man doing?'

'I don't know. It looks like he's feeding the pigeons.'

'But Mummy, he's trying to pick one up. There's blood. I think he's squeezing it.'

'Don't look.'

The father, Salman, who had been reading a London guidebook, looked up to see what was going on. 'No, Sunil is right, he's squeezing the bird! He's crushing the poor thing! Oh my God, what is he doing?'

'Mummy, I'm scared!'

As Chaz let the bird go, it flapped away and banged into the window. Salman, Sunita, and Sunil stared, open mouthed. Chaz looked up, panting in panic and, for the first time, noticed them. He gestured with his bloody hand, to the child, that they should shield his eyes or distract him. He mimed wringing the pigeon's neck, so they would understand.

'Aaargh! Mummy!'

By now, Salman had put down his book. 'He's thrown the fucking pigeon at us! What is he doing now?'

'I think he's threatening to kill us, Salman. Somebody, call the police! What if he tries to come in? HELP!' Pret staff and other customers were gathering at the window, terrified, sickened, yet mesmerised. The family fled their seats.

Shaking his head, Chaz carefully attempted to coral the panicked bird. He realised now that the family did not understand what was going on. But he owed a duty to the poor, suffering beast. He pinned it to the ground, clutched it in one hand, lifted it, and tried to ring its neck quickly and painlessly. Its head came clean off at the first twist.

Blood spurted over Chaz and the window. Everyone inside

took a step back. There were gasps. Two of the staff were moving stools to barricade the door, while the manager fumbled with the key. Several people filmed with their phones, and others were making calls.

'Mummy, are we going to die?'

'I told you we shouldn't come to London. It's just like in 'I', the place is full of gorre goons! And now we're going to be murdered here, like that Sikh couple!'

A man dashed over the road to Chaz. 'What the fuck are you doing, mate?' Sirens wailed in the distance.

Dolly sloughed off the scorched, ragged fleece. 'Fuck!' She looked to Starbuck.

THIS PAGE IS INTENTIONALLY LEFT BLANK

THE OBSIDIAN PIGEON

'Where are you from?'

'London.'

'I thought you were English when I heard your voice. So, how come you're selling this, then?'

'Shit happens. Sometimes things go wrong.'

'Mm, at least you're not foreign. How much are they?'

'Two pound fifty.'

'I'll take one, please.'

The day wore on. Annie supposed maybe our place in our story was the real help for the real problem. 'I love the paradox. Our truth makes us, and we make our truth. I'll stick with Jesus, thanks. It's a story that I hope and believe helps me change for the better.' I made a face. 'We could trade convincing arguments,' she went on, 'but I suspect neither of us is really open to persuasion.' She asked whether I was not experiencing a clash of different narratives. And should that not push us all to try and integrate them or find a better way of looking at it? I was not sure. We do crave a flow, some consistency. We shall continue, for the moment, to chase Blake's buttocks. What, for example, had happened to my baldness, my tan, my long hair? What happened to Byzantium and Troy—and how has our search for Troy gone so badly wrong? Why did I not care when my mother died? In time, narrative imperative must wring it out of the pages, surely? What of the black lamb? I will tell you a bit more, on account. It returned to Old Compton Street one spring afternoon. That was the same day I saw a tourist trip over an obdurate London pigeon, coming out of Pret. He fell flat on his face and spilled coffee over the pavement. The Lamb was in better form this time since, though both eyes had healed shut, it was confidently helping Todd to the door of a pub. Once he was in, the Lamb gambolled down to the Dairy.

It is a shop that sells cheese. To the initiated, on the other hand, it offers a trek round to the alley, to the Stilton den; that wretched hole where people lie on dirty mattresses thrown on the ground, revelling in the first sweat, the first flooding of the sinuses.

God of the socks, ye came to me on Long Acre under the gaze of your Virgin issuant from a bank of cloud, couped at the shoulders, proper vested in crimson and adorned all gold, her neck bejewelled, her beauty crined about the temples with a chaplet of roses alternately argent. Down the road the laughers laughed at the sub-god of the golden plates, while the living, breathing W. H. Smith trolled up Shaftesbury Avenue in the company of Miss Ryman to visit St. Giles's graveyard.

The Sun would shine and the rain rain, over and over. No-godders, the humaniness of humans might be comfort enough for you, while curiosity got the better of me. Some twist had taken place. There had been a change. I started out berating seekers of confession and absolution—the separate species and the looking down. In this next breath, it is I who am compelled to ask what the story is, and I who remain uncertain whether anybody really needs to know. I, who claimed to have long since ceased to Aunt Nell the cackling fakement of the Duchess Gloria mincing in my garden. But all there was to go on were fragments. Inside the horse, in the belly of this brazen bull, under some boat's benches or from the bowel of this juggernaut, all I heard was muffled, undetermined reality drop and jut. The roughness of my journey, the stifling confinement of that juddering boxcar, yielded only hints.

Consequently, as a tentative start, I warned my customers to gird their loins and set to questioning what they understood by the slogan written on our vendors' vests, our magic tabards: Working not Begging. Imagine if HSBC's strapline was 'Safeguarding not Stealing', or the Metropolitan Police were 'Protecting not Threatening'. My council of clients, then, my customers—many now friends—started coming on board. We went online together - launching a group chat. We kwebbelled on the pitches together. Together we would surely be able to make sense of it.

Legend has it the Duchess appears in many forms and was once a child who held a mountain aloft on a single lupper. Did Yu-Baaba help? The sweet redeeming sound, it is said, wafted over Jane's stream with a birdie. Nor dare I touch on the questionability of a snickering cave-fairy; playing with that got Sal so badly fingered by whiskered hypocrites for so long, all fancy dress and foul tempers. Whatever I believe or anybody does or does not believe, a lot of the duchesses are established franchise operations. Gloria, I meet people, only people, who praise you. Are you for real, or for real but a demiurge? All your best fans share a firm understanding that you are either actively intervening in human affairs to make things happen or allowin' things to happen and waitin' on us when we peg out. We both know I could no sooner sit down to tea with you than take Pret a Manger on a date and fondle it in an alleyway, but that makes neither of you any less human.

Don't be hard on George. Imagine, if you will, the lady

pushing her whole truth in a supermarket trolley. There is a hair's breadth, the width of a cigarette paper, between her and the acclaimed academic, the feted polymath. She may be a former English teacher driven mad by her pupils. She may have children who love her but cannot reach her, or she perhaps them. The brain is somewhat of a hedgehog; it passes through books, through experiences, through the world, catching bits and pieces on its quills. An idea here, some information there, a dream, a hope, a fantasy. That is what George has done. He has snuffled greedily about the hedgerows of philosophy, the ditches of logic, in the gardens of academia. He has crossed, barely scathed, the motorway of the Internet and the layby of... The layboy... The ladyboy... The... Oh, for fuck's sake. Tolkien is to be lauded for his detestation of metaphors. Unfortunately, I am wantonly, undiscerningly, enthralled by them.

I shouldn't join in, really, because so much literature, especially academic writing, is bloated with metaphorical detour, which it truly should not be. The posher the writer, the more likely the journey will take in that theme park of Hellenistic imagery which, according to the German swami, provides 'the shortest possible road to a clear cognitive understanding of behaviour different from our own.' Leaving aside the notion of there being an 'our own' behaviour, the question is this: when an anthropologist like Turner dances in Dionysiac abandonment at a Rio Carnival, is his metaphor truly used properly as a tool to convey some deep archetypal truth? Might most metaphor not simply be a lazy attempt to shape experience into conveniently recognisable stories? Scratch my balls. You've got to wonder, though.

THE MUFFIN MAN

Le chapelet du hasard

If the beads are disordered, yet you pray them all five times, have you prayed a Rosary?

What is gleaned, what accretes in the hedgehog's mind, is scraps and motes and snippets. Mouldering crab apples of wisdom are there. There are chocolate bar wrappers, along with fragments of polystyrene. This is the mental repository, the jumble that informs the collage presented as George. The first time I stood on Carnaby Street, trying to sell, it was like being caught in the wildebeest stampede in Lion King. Some of the elements make sense in the way that, say, a trout mask over a face on an album cover might, or Hannah Hoch's madchen. There may be disturbing, disjointed elements. There may be too many Oxford commas scattered, or too few. Trainer-slapped streets.

Forgive George; indulge him. He will lash out at times. He is offensive, occasionally sexist. He is angry, frustrated, infuriated at times. He feels judged, analysed, examined, measured, patronised, abused, and looked down upon. I feel I must apologise for myself, my predicament, because you have investigated the soul of my book and found it to be a shambles. The toys in my brain and heart box are spilled on your floor, and you are noticing bits of cat litter and shit, soiled nappies and cigarette butts among the Lego and broken Diecast cars. But this is what it is like in here. Slightly more worrying is that, amid the English teacher's trolley garbage, you discern moments from your own past and future. Put this book down, look around your room. The rock is the plate left uncleared after tea, the dust that can wait a bit. The hard place is the over-polished mirror and that thing which must be perfectly positioned. What do you expect of me? This is my English teacher's nightmare.

I fished out the photograph just now. The one from the times when people took photographs. It speaks to me of that other place; that land of lost content where I was a strapping teenager singing with a guitar. In the photograph I am gold-brown; falling to my shoulder, a mane of black ringlets, light revealing auburn here and there. My smile is a radiance of matched-pearl teeth. Neither do I recall when it was taken nor what I was singing. I cannot retrace my steps down the rolling mazy road that led me here, but that young man is still me, now, in my heart's heart.

The more I think, the less I need to feel.

Sad. We nutters are seldom geniuses, but many of us have delusions of it. You know the wisecracking knowing look drunk who talks complete shit yet esteems his wisdom to equal that of Solomon? The teenager who believes herself a cross between Pythagoras and Confucius, the result being streams of utter bollocks? Naturally, all typically cryptic in the cheapest register, pretending to know the secrets of the totality of facts, of things, of what is the case.

Here we have George Sanders sneering at the foot.

Funnily enough, incoherence and unintelligibility are significant impediments to successful authorship. Two considerably greater impediments are poverty and prejudice. What is it they know in arcane leers? Are they confiding, or taunting?

A passing visionary shared his wisdom. He believed 'they' were using telepathy to cause him to have accidents, listening to his speech, observing his actions. He was painfully aware this might appear odd, but felt confident telling me, since I obviously empathised (I did. After all, I wander among demons daily). On parting, he promised to pray direct to his god for me, and to do his best to ignore or shrug off telepathic interventions by the 'authorities' which caused him annoyance and mishaps. He believed this to be some great experiment, rather than specifically malicious or aimed personally at him; at least, that is the understanding he left me with. Unless he just meant to spread alarm and despondency.

Would this fellow and his story not have mothers herd their children away to safety? Would he offer his virgin daughter to strangers, or let them rape and dismember his maid? This, confirmed by those I told of the encounter and others who were present, all of whom considered Accident Man bonkers. What I reckon must have happened is that God made the world because he got lonely in the cold, empty vastness of pre-existence; lonely, and possibly a bit scared. Perhaps, as Menocchio puts it, out of the chaos our four elements— earth, air, fire, and water—mixed and created a mass, much as cheese is churned into solidity from milk, and worms appeared in it, and these were God and the angels.

When I eventually reached Holborn, the light was already fading. One of those nights when exposed fingers fuse and stiffen to become useless flippers. There was already a vendor on the Sainsbury's pitch, so I went to the Underground station. Had not been there five minutes when I was moved on by a plain clothes policeman. Bizarre. Crowds mooing, baaing, milling, me miles from the tube entrance he claimed I was blocking. It was cold. Steam billowed from mouths; even from your head if you took off your warm hat. He had a go at the poor Evening Standard people, too. This policeman was in a foul mood. I heard from other vendors that this same officer has a bee in his bonnet about Big Issue sellers. I looked over the road. Seeing that pitch now vacant, I harrumphed back to Sainsbury's, only to have a squinting beggar rise in ire from a palliasse formed of his worldly possessions, next to the cash machines—haggard genie—and aggressively order me to move. I was disrupting his custom.

Sooooo, I swore at him and marched off, in an even bigger huff. I felt all self-righteous, persecuted, and especially insecure. I knew, for example, the policeman was being a twat for no reason. Of course, whatever he says or does will be held to be Gospel over anything from my side, just as Roget trumped Paris so there is no recourse, no arguing whether he be right or wrong with knobs on. With the beggar, I did not mind so much his complaining, but his aggressive manner annoyed me. My departure was a triumph of blustering hysterical ineffectuality. To be honest, I flounced away like an angry six-year-old!

There we were; this policeman, me, and the beggar, jealously vying to control a bit of pavement we each felt to be our rightful territory—protecting our entitlements. Really, we should have held a pissing contest. To smell whose odours would win out. To learn who could spout higher, further, more voluminously. When I put this to one of the shop workers from Covent Garden, she told me I shouldn't bother with Holborn. 'Come back to Long Acre! We miss seeing you here on your piece of pavement. It feels like home having you outside our shop!' But I never pissed against her shop, so there must be more to it than scent-marking the space. Sometimes people told me I smelled. I would stand firm, strike my fists on my chest and yodel.

The real hard stuff is £25 an ounce, but who eats an ounce of cheese? So, that's £100 for any meaningful fix. It takes a whole lot of selling to carry a four-cheeses-a-week monkey. That's just the Stilton.

Christmas came surfing in on a savage westerly wind. Little Saint Nick on crack. 'I bought that one already' could not possibly be true so early on Monday morning, when you obviously had not bought a Big Issue. A handful might have, but I was intrigued by those who had not. There is no obligation to buy, apart from one people construct in their own imaginations. A body could just walk by and nod or say, 'No, thank you.' So many reasonably do. I puzzled over what brings out the 'I already have it' gambit.

What, for example, motivated the sultry Latin beauty— horny, tawny-tan stick, to slow to a haughty strut in the cool street, lift her chin, raise her eyebrows and her eyes under closed lids? What made her wag a chiding metronome finger at me in disapproval, puckering her lips into a perfect sphincter of disdain? All by way of response to my bidding her 'Good evening.'

Jenny, who worked in the Ugly Betty building, confessed in an email: 'I have sometimes falsely claimed to already have a Big Issue out of a basic approval-seeking desire. It's a way to manipulatively, duplicitously come across as good while still saying no. That is unless the vendor has totally busted the lie. Also, there is a shit-ton of guilt, so while there is no objective obligation a lot of people feel it anyway. Why guilt doesn't

catalyse into constructive action is a constant mystery to me.'
Jenny, how refreshingly honest.

I had, at the time, entered into a temporary rent agreement. The first sentence read: *This Agreement does not give, and is not intended to give, security of tenure.* From week to week, I might be told, that is TOLD, to move, at a week's notice. But at least I had a hostel roof over my head. It gets better. A little while before that, I had a similar room right by the Olympic Park East Village, still under construction. (DRUM ROLL) I was told homeless people are 'not eligible' to bid, nor apply to rent there. Needless to say, here we have yet another battle won on the playing fields of Eton.

'Waterloo?' I looked up. A bland man in a grey suit stood before me. 'Waterloo? Is that what you said?'

'Sorry?'

'You were talking about battles being won on the playing fields of Eton. I thought you might have meant the Battle of Waterloo.'

'I was saying that out loud?'

'I believe you were.'

He bought a Big Issue. I saw that I had moved fifty yards away from Pret. I hadn't even noticed, and still the rain fell and still I got it myself. Yes.

I got it... this vendor paranoia, periods when I felt too high a proportion of passers-by was deliberately ignoring me or giving disparaging looks. For my part, I usually let it roll over me. You could be Brigitte Bardot standing there naked, and people would still pass you, oblivious in their bubbles. Now many even stop up their ears, spending their days with background music further insulating them. It is easy to see how this can become a typical pitch feeling. It makes you defensive, and it can be hard to readjust when somebody is then unexpectedly nice.

'They're igrunt... They are orrible people. Totally harrogant!' was grumpy Brummy Wally's verdict. I cannot connect the phenomenon to the weather, although it appeared particularly liable to strike on slow days when money was short. Here's a thing: when you really, really need the money (you do always, but sometimes it is critical to meet immediate needs), time liquifies; it slows, and the magazines cling to you like forlorn waifs. 'We love you. Please protect us and keep us. We NEVER want to leave you.' Usually if it is a slow day, everybody is having one, and vendors who know they will not be able to dispose of all their mags seek to offload them, at cost, onto other vendors, who are not sure of selling them, either. A general desperation to get rid of books sets in.

It was on such a Monday that a man who had gone by me for a year, with, I had assumed, an air of disdain, not so much as casting me a glance, turned and walked back ten paces after passing to say, 'I always go by you and never buy a Big Issue. I don't read it.' Then he handed me a tenner, with a big smile. Equally inscrutable, a woman from the Ugly Betty building who, after months of passing and paying me no heed, began nodding in acknowledgment, then, out of the blue, started buying me cups of tea in the morning and a sandwich at lunchtime, only to suddenly stop after a few weeks. She then spent months awkwardly blanking me, like an ex who had dumped me, until my unflagging, cheery hellos brought her back round to nodding acknowledgement. It's as predictable as volcanoes.

Once you get the hang of Carnaby Street, it's not too bad. You need to stand in the flow, in the centre of the street—which is s pedestrianised—like a Kodiak grizzly snatching for salmon. On any pitch, if you stand too long in the cold weather, your legs can get a bit shaky.

Fuck you, fuck your mother, fuck everything about you. How dare you give me, a stranger, a bitten bap and a half-drunk bottle of water. Of course, that's not what I say - I say 'Thank you.'

I spotted Burning Ben, out of the corner of my eye, passing at the end of the street. It was him, for sure. He was unmistakable. Yes... Please... No. Thank you very much... Fuck off! And it was, as for Carl, a flip dark chill winter bastard of a night, when some young lads set upon Eddie. Welsh Eddie who was drunk. He was not scared and put his dukes up to them. They beat him up bad. But it was Ben, two streets away in that same dark, who fell victim to the evening-dress arsonist.

I met Dolly in St Paul's Churchyard just as Victor took his leave of her. Curious, Victor hated druggies and drunks, yet I often saw him in Dolly's company.

'I made it myself.'

'What?'

'Myself, I suppose. This, what I'm made of. I made it myself.'

'How do you mean?'

'I found this big Irish head by the Tower, and the body is Dan the Jew. He said I could have it.'

'Oh, right.'

'See, I could sort of bring the body back to its boxing shape, although it, and the head, are a bit battered. But George, I'm telling you this because I need your help.'

'How's that?'

'I need you to help me capture the Lamb. I must have the Lamb.'

Inveterate liar.

Many who passed were extremely kind, polite. I heard 'Get a job!' comments and sarcasm oftener from Cockney youths. Don't get me wrong; most, even of the Cockney men, were perfectly civil and many bought the mags but, of the hecklers, they were the majority. 'No thanks, mate. Me shoes fit perfectly! Fnar, fnar.'

Marge put it down to insecurity. 'If not for Mummy's and Daddy's pension that funds their lifestyle, they know they would be swapping places with you. They are vocalising fear.' Maybe the same fear that led the nob to set fire to Ben. It was twelve years ago in an alleyway off Strand.

Aye, Christmas went, and Martin rolled along. He had visited his ex a couple of weeks before the holiday, in Kent, which he described as being 'somewhere near Basingstoke, sure.' His ex put him up, and he seemed much the better for it; in colour, general fullness, and disposition.

'I've given up the flat. I told 'em I can't stay there. It don't feel right.' His eyes misted with some hopeful vision. 'I could live in a HOUSE. A proper place, yes, with a bit of a yard. I gave them back the keys.' He was back to sleeping rough, waiting for his key worker and others to meet to discuss a way forward.

The beach is empty; corbeaux, osprey, and all the feathered terrors gone with the last red-gold rays of Sun. Timid crepuscular hermit crabs begin to appear. They carry shells, bits of rubbish, back and forth along the strand. One tiny crab carries a toothpaste cap for shelter. The beach becomes busier as night descends. A crab discards a too-small shell, having found a more commodious alternative. In turn, smaller beasts size-up, each scuttling to find a place to forage or bed down in the warm sand or vanish into the surf to sleep among the coral. It turns suddenly colder. The Moon rises above gently swaying palms, its sodium orange sphere glowing bright. Each crab humps its cardboard burden, sleeping bag or blanket, up and down Strand, eventually taking to the water and swimming until it finds a doorway, an alleyway, where more skilled, more experienced reef-dwellers will fashion a Toblerone, safe among the anemones. Some parts of the reef have developed spikes to keep off vagabond crustaceans. Others emit spray, display radiant colours, make annoying noises. But there is enough room on the reef for all the fish, and Ben eventually settles in a doorway down an alley, sheltered from the battering breakers of the outer reef wall and noisy traffic.

Blue fish do be fickle. Sometimes they will ward off predators, other times they may nab you themselves. Overall, blue fish leaves you alone if you keeps out their way, their presence is almost reassuring. Of all predators, the crabs fear liberal fish most; once they catch their prey, they painfully and slowly understand it to death. On this night, the blue fish were elsewhere. Why Ben dossed alone, away from others, is bare mysterious. Nonetheless, he was awakened at three in the morning by a stream of piss rattling on his sturdy tube. Peak, but not too problematic; the box was stout and if he played dead the lout would soon get bored and wander off. Perhaps he was too drunk to even know there was anybody under the cardboard. Ben lay still, quiet, patient—he and his fellow crabs' usual way of escaping attention from the relentlessly curious, voraciously omnivorous beach barbie-goers.

The lout clearly did know. A new liquid splattered. But this was brandy; Ben could smell that... What the? Scratch, hiss, whoosh! Too late, Ben struggled to rid himself of his cocoon, but got tangled in the sleeping bag, which was the problem. He might have shrugged off burning cardboard; torn his way out of it, but the fucking sleeping bag clung like a mummy's bandages, searing into his flesh. The smell was dreadful. The yob stood over him, a youth. Initial laughter gave way to blind panic. He took off his own coat and dinner jacket and tried to beat out the flames. 'Fuck, NO! Fuck NO!' But Ben did not go out.

'What have you done?' Ben pleaded. 'What have you DONE?' He lurched toward the lad, making a grab, but was too slow. Snatching his coat back, with its sparking, smouldering seams, the trembling arsonist fled toward the bustling confusion that is Covent Garden. Benny kept on burning... Nobody called the fire brigade; nobody saw.

Not everyone can perceive it. There is a bit of visible keloid scarring and to the face and neck, and that is all. If they could see the twisted waste land of his torso, what would they say? Yes, Ben is *still* on fire now—he will never go out. You can make out the flames that envelop him and trail him when he moves. You can feel heat from him. Blue wisps of smoke curl from his mouth and nostrils. His eyes glow like coals, he smells of caramelised Christmas pudding and singed hair.

Somewhere in Esher, a married man wakes with a jolt at three every Sunday morning. Sometimes he screams himself awake. The dream is always the same: there comes a knock at the front door. Even though he knows who it is, he is compelled to answer. When he does, when he opens the door, there is a rush of heat from the burning tramp on the step, endlessly pleading, 'What have you DONE?' The man's wife is often annoyed by his reluctance to go into the West End to see a show or have a night out. What can this married father and loving husband say to her? What can he do now to fix it? What purpose would be served by owning up? It would not stop his troubled conscience consuming him in flames every bit as bright as Ben's.

This man will never join the parade of girl mahouts on their fathers' shoulders, goading them up Long Acre, of boy tyrants and their doting mothers on that magic roundabout. Kaleidoscopic humanity with all its inexplicable hurriedness.

There goes everybody, rambling up and down and back and forth. At last, a riposte to my 'Big Issue?'

'No, mate. The Big Issue is me travelling through time to prove God exists!' Those were his exact words. He clearly was not joking. A youngish bloke.

Two other fellows answered my offer with, 'No, mate. We're workmen.' Which they obviously were, but what is the connection between being a workman and not being interested in buying The Big Issue?

'No, mate. I can't read!' I was tempted to believe that one.

Big Issue vendors go out in all weather. Sometime in the bleakness after Christmas, there was a Build Your Vendor a Shop competition, to get readers to goodthink of vending more as a business and see what they could come up with by way of a stand, or portable selling point. The trouble with this, from us vendors' point of view, was that it was more like Build Your Vendor a Cage. We reckoned it would restrict us on the pavement. We would effectively be tethered like goats and ultimately have more trouble selling mags. Had people not heard of umbrellas? Small black frilly ones, even?

You find yourself saluting magpies and buying lottery tickets. You check payphones and tube ticket machines for coins. Then you look around, and it is your own child, skeletal by the dry village pump, with flies crawling on her face.

There was a lot of vying for pitches in those times, whether Christmas swooped before or behind us, with the days getting bigger. Essentially, you could only book a pitch—that is, get first 'dibs' on it—if you sold more than five and thirty magazines a week. You would have to take potluck otherwise. It is not so simple. There were lots of vendors established on pitches before the 35 mags rule who did not, and could never, for various reasons, sell that many magazines. What do you do? We vendors commonly call the magazines 'books' but never 'silver darlings.'

Aden said, 'Hopefully, Big Issue management will drop that rule soon when they find out how unpopular it is amongst vendors.' His optimism was misplaced. The women from the jeweller's shop gave me a belated Christmas card, which was sweet of them. Aden had a ruddy farmer tan, broad, strong hands, fair, springy hair. He saw the lands beyond Albion's shores as full of inferior native folk who could never live up to the magnificence of John Bull, whose equal no one has ever met. That said, he had a keen awareness of the fight for rights and justice waged by British workers through history, in the context of a world struggle. He was also an enthusiastic PEGIDA and UKIP supporter.

Target or no for The Big Issue, one regular of mine, a tall, balding Cockney, had targets. His name was Bill. Like myself, no sales, no pay. Bill was a peripatetic purveyor of wholesale meat to the catering trade, in which capacity he schlepped wearily from restaurant to restaurant to big business. Bill had had a glum Christmas: sadly, his father died, and he and his wife (they had no children) were penurious. He suffered with stress-induced psoriasis. Now he and his wife must wait for his father's estate to be settled, to recoup the funeral costs. He was a real hero for buying The Big Issue, being skint himself. He knew my circumstances, which are never a secret to anybody who asks.

Bill said he found our chats therapeutic, which was mutual; I enjoyed our meetings. He was amazed that I was so cheerful, but I joked (although it was not really a joke) that he had never seen me with my mother when she was alive! We always had a good chinwag when he passed, once a month. He was used to meeting me on Long Acre and surprised when he met me on a different pitch. It was disorientating. 'It threw me a bit,' he said.

The people at Pret, Broadwick Street, informed me that for the first time since I started going there, months ago, there had been a different vendor at their door. The Barista got 'territorial' and defensive when the man came in to ask for coffee (which I would never do). He even teased the vendor before giving it to him. My happy conclusion is that, over the short space of a couple of months, the Pret people came to view me as their Big Issue vendor, like the people in the shops on Long Acre and I, reciprocally, felt like their Big Issue vendor. I must again make it clear: I never scent marked the pavement outside Pret nor had they scent marked me on behalf of the shop. Thus, it was not the geur of the strange vendor that made them wary of him. Although, it could have been. Had I found out who he was, I might have jumped him and kicked him to death in an alley. No, I would not have, honest. I jest; I be only joking. We glued a twenty pence piece to the pavement. Watching people try to pick it up gave me, the couriers and the Pret staff a bit of a laugh.

Is anything of the tedium being conveyed here? The emptiness? Est-ce vraiment que le sujet s'éloigne toujours du verbe, et que le complément direct vient chaque fois se poser quelque part dans le vide? Probably. Nor is it only language that disjoints. Not just words, but whole intellects, whole civilisations may evaporate in ennui. More often from broken equilibrium. Worlds slide down the gullet of the greedy only to rain back down on them as their own shit. Existence is brutal, crude. We get comfortable even in despair. We clothe ourselves in self-pity and wait to be poked back into action. We can't cook, we won't cook; we've never seen a cookbook. There's fast food, takeaways, and snacks—why get up off our lazy backs? We'd rather starve than stir a pot. We'd rather leave fresh food to rot. What budget? Us? Yeah, right. No thanks. We much prefer to use food banks. My need for love and acknowledgement is insatiable. My hubris and self-loathing wrestle constantly on this seesaw.

As I wrote above, and may echo ad nauseum, it was my way to ask for nothing, never ever. Though I would offer the paper to anyone who wanted to just give me money, I seldom refused random cash. 'Working not Begging.' When people gave too much for the mag, I saw it kind of, sort of, in the manner of, like a doorman, waitress or cabbie getting tips, my service being to stand and offer The Big Issue. 'Do not tip our waiting staff. It insults them!'

'We strongly advise against giving presents to the lollipop lady at the end of term; it only encourages her.'

'Do not embarrass our politicians by subsidising second homes for them or giving them cheap food and transport. They, for their part, would much prefer to stand on their own lallies, their own dollies, ta much!' And people looking at me, even though I had my tabard on, and I realised I had shouted it: 'DO NOT EMBARRASS OUR POLITICIANS!' I repeated it. People were staring.

Welcome to my pavement. Please feel free to walk on by, stop for a chat, or buy a magazine. Thank you for visiting. Have a nice day. Of course, I believe you will 'get one on the way back.' You probably believe it yourself, until you encounter the angel who tells you to go back some other way. You will not beat your donkey either, nor will she rebuke you.

As sometimes happens, an old acquaintance chanced upon me, and somewhat nonplussed, stopped to talk. When I told him I had been vending over a year, he asked why I 'chose' to become a Big Issue vendor in the first place. 'I mean, what's your motivation for taking up this particular challenge?' The penny had not dropped for him. I explained that the challenge is being homeless in reality. He was not sure how to respond. Tears welling in his eyes, he gave me £10 'for old times' sake.' And hurried away, bemused, upset. The wind howls. A thousand people shuffle by and one or two stop. The dust blows... Listening to those mouse toes... When am I gonna die? When I stop waiting? When you stop reading? Is it that they are scrabbling in the ceiling? Put down your cheese, put down your chicken leg, take up the axe, and go see.

Shortly after the erstwhile friend left, a chap passed me twice in the space of ten minutes. He walked by in the same direction both times. My strong feeling is that, for reasons best known to himself, he walked, swam, climbed, and jumped in a roughly straight line, circumnavigating the globe in that short window of opportunity—which for him took eleven years, three months, thirteen days, eighteen hours, and seventy-five minutes. It is no business of mine what cruel debt or quirk of circumstance drove him to undertake such a perilous adventure. Given he never bothered me, I would not presume to express an opinion regarding his stunt. In those years while he journeyed, his wife re-married and he was blessed with a grandchild. We went to war with Iraq on the day he began parkouring out of the Moscow suburbs and leaping hedges toward Poland. Somehow, even though he stopped not to bathe, not to eat, not to drink, and shamelessly relieved himself on the hoof, his dungarees remained as tidy as when I first saw him. He had not grown a beard to go with his moustache, and he still held the same pristine, unused paintbrush and unopened pot of yellow paint in his left hand, clutching the crisp pink trade invoice in his right. I take my hat off to that man. He is a scholar and a priest in my book. It was all I could do to hold myself back from rushing up to him, shaking his hand and embracing him for his integrity and determination, saluting him for his strength, his courage, his indefatigability.

THE DRESSING-DOWN

I was further prevented from approaching him by a well-dressed woman in her forties who bought a Big Issue. She asked after my 'situation.' I told her. 'So, you're not actually homeless, then?' I said that hostel places are not homes, and pointed out a nearby fellow vendor, saying politely that he most definitely was sleeping on the street, and she should feel free to go to him, I would not be in the least put out. She said she had started buying from me and would get it from me, even though the money was being denied a 'real' homeless person.

One of my shop workers, a mother, when she read in my blog of this encounter, wrote that she had recently 'faced over fifteen months of housing insecurity. Even without at any stage being likely to end up without a roof over our heads, I now realise what a HUGE stress it is not to know where you will be, when you move, what will happen.' She added that it was 'Exhausting! Good job I haven't had to put up with people making judgements like that. I might have given her a rolled-up copy over the head.' I was thinking more along the lines of exacting justice by cursing the woman, that she might be afflicted with homelessness or torn apart by bears. But I feared Abigail might denounce me as a warlock. Instead, she wrote: 'It's not hard to be forgiving. It comes naturally and benefits you twice as much as the recipient. It is an awesome quality, almost divine. So, George, rather than seeking justice, look to mercy, because justice is a levelling down; mercy, a levelling up. Take care, too, because justice may leave you with one eye!'

THE MUFFIN MAN

Kevin had not long finished a volunteer role with The Big Issue. He now felt safe to write: 'I volunteered for the last four months. Being a member of The Big Issue street team, I spent it mostly out on the streets of London, visiting vendors te ouwehoeren, and see if they had any questions or issues that we at The Big Issue might be able to help with. I'll tell you, George, one of the things that struck me most is the remarkable degree of specialised geographical knowledge vendors developed of their surrounding areas, and the clever techniques, tradecraft might be a good way of describing it, of making urban spaces more hospitable.' That put me in mind of Charlie Store, a vendor in Richmond, Yorkshire, who sells in the shadow of the Castle. His specialised geographical knowledge, published in The Big Issue Magazine, was that: 'I can see the Castle, but I've never actually been in it.' I'll give you odds of eighty-nine to three that if Bryan ever enquires whether he might visit the castle, he will be told, 'No! Neither now nor at any other time!'

I once overheard Kevin in conversation with Burning Ben, who described in detail the best way to make a Toblerone resistant to the elements. Several thin layers on the bottom, a half box at either end, an awning of sorts over the top, which also made the shelter easy to exit quickly, should the need arise. Ben did not elaborate why this might be a useful feature. That it was drizzly made obvious the need of an awning. Another vendor interrupted to tell Kevin that, in his experience, car parks provided an excellent haven during cold winter nights. He went on to explain that they were easily accessible at night, through various entrances, always dry, heated by air vents from the building, and brightly lit.

Children saw. 'Mummy, why is that man on fire?' When it rained, Ben would hiss, steam, and smoke. As it happens, I had been given a better umbrella, and lent Ben the black frilly one. He would not get wet.

How do we feel about bus-stops? Cigars, I smoke thousands. I usually deal in the Strand.

Like the essential crafts of fashioning cigars and cigarettes from discarded stubs, building gondolas by hand in Venice, or thatching, this practical, unique, and specialised body of knowledge—that is, how to construct urban one-person shanties—is passed from individual to individual, generation to generation. I reminded Kevin that it has been this way for hundreds of years. Even before Burlington Bertie from Bow. There has been a homeless 'community' in Covent Garden and Strand since before there was a Strand. But you've got to take care when you're getting them there, the cigars. Kevin had something. Newcomers are commonly taken under the wing of older, more seasoned street people.

I asked what he thought of the tabards, the phenomenon of vendors. He said: 'One of the perspectives I see when I observe someone selling a magazine on the street is a series of commodifications. The Big Issue magazine is a commodity which vendors are looking to sell. The red tabard, with its slogans, commodifies character traits, such as self-reliance and obstinacy.' His left eye twitched. 'These are characteristics which potential customers are encouraged to reward through buying a magazine. In purchasing, the customers, perhaps, are able to buy into the idea of doing some charitable deed. That might make them feel good.' He pointed to my tabard. 'The tabard itself has an advert on the lower back—an advert for

THE MUFFIN MAN

Fairhills, a wine company; an interesting choice of sponsor.'

We are commodities selling commodities. Perhaps we should all wear kilts. Redemption through work. Yep, really.

The observation that vending is vaguely Pavlovian was sharp. He missed the bit where, in this economy of salvation, each book sold takes a flake of soul and spark for every spoonful of self-confidence it instils. The paradigm of elevating exchange—this contract, this bargain—is bang in line with the stereotype of vendor: consideration does not need to be adequate, nor even tangible. Neither did Kevin hear the voice in the midst of the four beasts repeat, 'A measure of wheat for a penny, and three measures of barley for a penny; and thou hurt not the oil and the wine.' Then, he didn't notice Benny being on fire, either.

The day the Earth stood still

In late winter, we had Haydn Gwynne, Aleister Crowley, and Alison Steadman on Covent Garden pitches, selling the magazine as part of a project called Stageswap. Volunteers get a briefing beforehand from The Big Issue Foundation and turn up to us mid-morning. Being famous, the three of them sold lots of mags, even in the rain. People were surprised, some a little scared, to see Aleister vending in his plus-4 suit and gaiters. Most people thought he was Noël Coward, which did not amuse him. The myrrh overtones of his Abramelin oil lent him a certain priestly quality, though not obscuring the grave stench. He flattered Alison by asking 'Alright, Ange?' Such a charmer. I complimented him on his Thoth brooch.

I took him to meet Dolly the Hat. They hailed each other

as friends, joked, laughed, and shared the rustiest, most hideous needle I have ever seen. The amount of heroin they took between them would have killed a regiment of normal addicts. Aleister boasted to Dolly that he had sold fourteen magazines. I pointed out this was ten fewer than Haydn or Alison. He confessed himself perplexed, but times change, the magic becomes fuzzy. He returned to his tomb to rest. Meanwhile, Aden says, 'Regular vendors did really badly because everyone bought a magazine from that dead bloke and the other celebrities. I think stunts like this by The Big Issue are a bad idea.'

We often held volunteer sessions, when people from other walks of life—say, offices—came to sell. Wouldn't it be great if there were little camels the size of cats? Wouldn't it be brilliant? There arose much bickering among vendors over who made the list to have volunteers on their pitch (we were paid in free magazines), with the office tending to pick from a sanitised roll of those who did not grump or complain, and not selecting new 'unknown quantity' vendors. I got picked a lot. Camels, whales, weasels. What's the difference? I've looked at that cloud from both sides now, but I still don't know fuck about it. And you will be my slave in the afterlife, or I yours. We will be shadows, imaginings, after the Man comes around, only he won't.

A fellow vendor had a territorial altercation with a tour guide, who halted his group at the man's pitch and proceeded to lecture them. When the vendor protested being crowded off the pavement, the guide tutted, 'I'm trying to work.' He complained to The Big Issue head office about said vendor! This was the same vendor who worked on the edge of the

City. After that, he covered his badge number, as the SPG used to. He said there are a great many people who 'hate vendors' and complain maliciously. He also came in for an inordinate number of 'get a job' jibes. We all got them, but his receiving shedloads was, I suspect, a function of the location of his pitch. Wake me up when we land... or if the trolley comes around, which it must, on this bitch of an earth.

Would I cut their balls off and use them to bait fish? People who take the piss, who scorn us, who read and write all sorts of shit about us—poverty porn, just because we're Big Issue vendors. But we have eyes, hands, a place in humanity's sweet cesspool. We eat, we dream, we get sick like everybody else and stand, our bits freezing, in the same winter as everybody else. We get food poisoning from cheap street burgers, and we die like everybody else. And some bastard thought it was alright to set fire to one of us! Is fight fire with fire the lesson to learn from that?

Patches, where something spilled on the carpet has dried. I tried ever and oftener to gather comments. Few, except partisans—the pro-vendors I loved and the anti-vendors I sought to fathom—would give opinions. It seems to me that, in the same way politics is carried on by a tiny number of inordinately active people, who end up deciding how we all live, society is carried (controlled?) by a minuscule, accidental, and fluctuating clique which exercises real power, while we all bumble in twilight. I hear heads echoing verbatim what they read in The Daily Hate as their own opinion. I hear their voices on the phone to that odious sarcastic freak on Radio Rant, jeering at those with no platform to respond. It is not a conspiracy; it is what societies churn up. When I get the dark glasses, I will look at strangers, the headlines, and posters to see if I see. There is something endlessly fascinating about the smell of burning hair.

Spring Thursday

Bendix was losing patience. The procession, always late, appeared to be terminally stalled. As she was about to call it a day, the doleful Lambeg struck up. At last.

Today, Spring Thursday, while still a solemn feast, is transformed. From the relentlessly dour history of spontaneous auto-amputations, of the faithful springing to their deaths, has emerged a dignified, stately day of elaborate procession and reflection. Auto-amputation, long illegal, is punishable by four years imprisonment. It has proven difficult to prosecute. Who is to say a worker fell in front of the lumber saw or freight wagon deliberately? Did the leg wound become infected by mischance? The loss of a limb in battle is seldom suspect, and soldier amputees are especially revered.

So it is that the Most Worshipful Column of The Leg, in their ancient black felt caps, red sleeved tunics, and gilded breastplates, lead the procession. Behind, the Lambeg and two pipers who traditionally walk. These musicians are followed by various orders of priests, brothers, and sisters, some of whom do not bind their right legs[1], but keep them raised as a token of faith for the duration of the circuit. Next come jinglers, led by white-clad tambourine players, in colourful costume, sporting ankle bells. Keeners, sometimes hundreds of them, make up the rear-guard. Later, the thousands of lay

---

1   The knee is held up in front of the springer by means of a sling.

springers would file past.

As the procession approached, Bendix lowered her gaze and raised her right foot. Being eight, she was not expected to stand on one leg the whole time. Children are also afforded the indulgence of folding the leg behind, rather than raising the knee. Ethel, Bendix's friend, belonged to a strict family, so she tried to keep her right knee proudly high as long as possible.

The Podiants, as Columnists are known, sprang to the Lambeg's beat in remarkable unison. An elderly Podiant in the front rank fell flat on her face. To Bendix's amazement, without missing a beat, the procession halted and sprang in place. Medics, who dot the route, dashed over, scooped up the faller and whisked her away. The faller's file sprang forward. The ranks being restored, a voice rang out: 'Foot To! Spring on!' The procession resumed.

This ceremony has taken place for seven hundred and fifty-seven years without interruption, although much has changed, and it was once a bloody spectacle. The original processions would leave town on the coastal road, past the ashheaps, to Galat's Rock and return by way of The Mount—a circuit of nearly seven furlongs, half of it up and downhill. In ancient times, smithies stood with axes, cauldrons of pitch and cauterising materials at the starting point, and the faithful would queue diligently. There are records of waist-high piles of severed legs. The modern route stays in town, a little under three furlongs, made possible when shards broke off from Galat's Rock during an earthquake. Four large splinters were gathered and erected around the town. Now only the most ardent pilgrims spring from the square to the Rock and back.

All over the square gaudy stalls and shops brim with images

and replicas of the shards and the Rock—keyrings, gewgaws, tea towels, statuettes. Galat's Rock and the shards are protected by stout glass enclosures, constantly guarded, yet credulous pilgrims still pay enormous sums for fresh slivers of the True Rock. Rock merchandise is eclipsed by that of Blessèd Anton himself. Anton Zamak—prophet, priest, king with the grey hypnotic eyes—is portrayed either raising his leg to kick the Tyrant or legless on his fateful journey to the Rock. But by far the dominant feature of shops, procession, and street decorations are the Blessèd Eyes. They hang from lantern posts, they stare from shelves and shop windows, adorn tee shirts, glare from the town crest on the library, on police cars, fire trucks, bollards. They are on bumper stickers. They are everywhere, keeping vigil. Even out of town, on the road to Galat's Rock, from a temple billboard, they peep over a pair of giant spectacles, above the words, 'Look Beyond!'

The clamour was deafening. Metal thunder; a huge engine's mighty crunch. The repeated monstrous crash made hair stand and blood rush to the face. This was Bendix's favourite part of the procession. When she was older, she hoped to be chosen as a tambourinist. A little way off in the crowd, Bendix noticed a stranger. She could tell he was foreign because of his peculiar legs: thin and symmetrical. Bendix was not the only one sneaking a peek. Though it was not expected of him, he gamely tottered on one leg, head bowed. Now and then he wavered and brought his right foot to the ground. It was a sterling effort. Granny's words came to her: 'Them's walks straight talks in circles.' At that moment, the foreigner caught her eye and smiled warmly. Bendix blushed. Granny was wise, told her not to be condemning Idiot Samuel, even though the whole town ridiculed and despised him. He and his brother had gotten drunk and amputated each other's legs. Brother Bill died, but when Sam came to, his heretical severed left leg greeted him—a harbinger of his new pariah status.

Eventually the Keeners came. Raising giggles from children and exasperated sighs from some of the elderly in the crowd, the foreigner turned clockwise. Bendix suppressed a grin as he caught her eye, this time in helpless puzzlement. At least he knew to turn his back. When to walk away was easy, he could follow the crowd. This was funniest of all. He set off with comical equilibrium. People stared open-mouthed, some laughed aloud. He did not care in the least. Step after jaunty step in a perfectly straight line. It was hard to believe and difficult to watch. Bendix could not contain herself; she laughed until her head and belly hurt. Then he approached. 'I shall never forget this. I am so glad I came. You have all been so welcoming.'

Again, she blushed. Bendix wondered whether she might see the stranger next month on Inclination Tuesday, more commonly called Leaning Day.

It is hard to pin George down; one moment he is Joel Cairo, Signor Ugarti, then less 'communistical' than Countess Kuchinska, and begging for sponsorship. Next, he is torn like Smeagol and Gollum, snapping, simpering, plotting viciously. All at once, he is Uriah Heap, Hans Christian Andersen on stilts and Hannibal Lecter but without the criminal genius.

'You should write a book.'

'Why don't you write a book?'

'There's a book to be written here.'

'You ought to write all this down,' is what people continually

say. But write what? Who wants to read about saying 'Big Issue' a thousand times a day for a thousand days? It is boring, it is drudgery. Not endowed with the eloquence of Steinbeck that turns despair into a painful but compelling challenge, nor with the parodic skills of a Rankin or a Pratchett, how is George to write? What publisher is going to give it a second glance? Struggling to justify your situation; not homeless enough for this one, not drug-addicted enough for that one, not stupid enough for many but with only a pastiche intellect and a carbuncle of a mind which no amount of draining can rid of poison.

Raoul Duke

Readability is one issue. There is also the question of style; to leave in errors, repetitions, to capture the gush of wanting to tell the tale. Or to keep the eccentricity but couch it more eruditely. Either way, the whole thing looks crazy. The first method, though—and this is what will happen with the first draft—will put off prospective publishers. They will assume all the peculiarities are errors. Everything serious in the book will be construed as comedy and every joke will be taken seriously.

Orwell anticipated something like it. Huxley had an angle on it. Foucault and Lukes tied it down even better. 'Social compliance' is, we read now, how a business protects the health, rights, and safety of their employees, supply, and distribution chain. Fucking hell.

Is this writing public masturbation?

George is a patent author surrogate. The whale in Moby Dick is not an author surrogate. There is an element of avatar in all characters, but George (oh the pretension!) is more of a

THE MUFFIN MAN

Meursault, an homme de Soho, than a Duke. A further difficulty arises regarding what George is purported to be channelling. It might be drivel. My man is walking around the West End, on his head, a gold orgone plated steel pyramid that is 'especially recommended for those new to Pyramid technology.'

The story of homelessness—the grand narrative, as it were—is disputed and woven by a handful of interested parties who effectively set dominant themes with which we, Nietzsche's noughts, tend to go along unquestioningly, or to which we offer little challenge. Is that cobblers? Is it right or trite? In the end, the boot on the face becomes calming; it is our boot, not some nasty invader's clog. I fear an imminent political or cod-philosophical diatribe may be... No, the moment has passed. I will diminish and go into the West. Meanwhile, let me continue to grope in the shadowy belly of this whale for some inkling of understanding through storytelling. And while we are at this impasse.

I asked my good customer Marigold why so few people share their views with me. While she herself was 'happy to see what goes on behind the smiles that you treat us to in Soho daily, I think life is full of people who do and people who do not, who can't, who wouldn't. If it's commenting or feeling they have anything useful to say. Or, like we discussed, helping others, finding time to do charity work or other things.' She shrugged. 'I often type, I read, delete depending on mood, confidence. I don't know, various obstacles...' Her words were lost to me. From the moment she stood by me, on The Land within these Brass Studs, her scent and the glorious vision of her cleavage had caught me, monopolised my mind. What should I say in defence? Should I have a defence? Need

I? If my bollocks were the size of grapefruit and grew from my chest, spilling over the top of my half-buttoned shirt, would the average woman not sneak a look? For whatever hormonal reason, my whole world was suddenly bounded by those smoothed bulges, the deep Romantic chasm between them. I held Patsy's breasts, I caressed them, I ejaculated over them and... then something happened that I had not expected, that eclipsed the delights of Petunia's much abused bosom. To my horror, it put me in mind of Aleister. It happened so unexpectedly that I stopped nodding and smiling. It was that I—and I am reluctant to share this, but must force myself—I realised I had a weak erection!

Panic set in. Swiftly, I reviewed my thoughts of the last few moments. Amber's rich, womanly reek filled my nostrils, her banana muffin breath, and the vanilla overtones of 'Daisy'. I could feel her warmth ebb and flow as we came closer or parted, her chest rising and falling pleasantly with her speech. By rights, given my sexual frenzy, I should have had a bulge, been obliged to focus on not cumming in my pants. But there it bobbed, a warm, cosy, half-meltiness. Tina, a super attractive twenty something, continued, 'I like to read too, and quietly watch without having to dig in and see what my own opinion is. I suspect that there are many people who do that because what you say is complete.' Which sounded like a polite way of telling me I do not let people get a word in edgeways.

By now I was frantically conjuring ever more perverse scenarios, unable to come to terms with a challenge to my libido. I nodded and gurgled as Fran bade me goodbye. Even after she turned to leave, I heaped sicker and sicker abuse on her anatomy in a forlorn bid to get stiff by the power of fantasy.

THE MUFFIN MAN

Was I tired? Was I unwell? Did I have an orgone deficiency? Might I have prostate or colon cancer? Blind terror, total hysteria, I spent the rest of the afternoon contemplating every living, breathing being that passed as a sex toy in an effort to erectify my penis betrayal. Badum, tssss!

That evening, as soon as I shut the door behind me, I lifted my coat and jumpers, pulled down my pants, and masturbated. To my continuing annoyance, I ejaculated half soft, after only two minutes, twenty-eight seconds, with no projection at all. Sperm too clear, not enough of it, spilled over my hand and balls out of this sorry, squiggly Quisling of a prick. I hated it and I hated myself. This was how I would be left, then, enduring a purgatory rancid with lust, with no way of having any real sex. I dusted off my copy of 'Funktion des Orgasmus'.

After a week of mustering the forces, as Kenneth would say, of frequent frenetic wanking, porn, auto-vegetotherapizing, and concentration on general human penetrability, affairs returned to normal. Portnoy would be proud of such a spurt (oh yeah, all the way up to the lightbulb? Come off it!). I almost cried with relief. But the writing was on the wall. Now, where was I?

ANTEROS

Winter sun poured over London. The tenth day. I did not work but went to Stanford's map shop to buy a book (that's for me to know). On the way, I visited Victor at his pitch, my pitch, on Long Acre. Victor the Sardinian. His English was perfect. Heavily accented. He wore a lapel pin—a tiny enamel fly.

Victor told me his family still resided on a farm in Sardinia, but some lived variously abroad. Victor himself once stayed in New York. His fortunes had been mixed. How to paint him? Greying, not quite bald, four foot seven, wiry, nervously energetic, slightly hunched. Here follows an over-description. His face receded into the wide shadow of an enormous overhanging forehead. From the middle of the face protruded a nose grown long and bulbous, trying to reach light, its tip forming the upper horn of a crescent that swept to his jagged lower horn of Habsburg chin. He had a scrawny neck, big ears. Hazel eyes, set immediately next to each other, darted as he talked. Bad teeth. Victor spoke in an insistent nasal whine; exaggerated, as though he were heroically struggling in the face of great odds, defying a hostile audience, yet gloating. His skin was pale and shiny. At whiles, he suddenly drew in close, confiding in conspiratorial whispers, all the time glancing about. He was presently staying in a safe, dry (no alcohol) hostel. He neither drank nor approved of it (he was religious). Victor kept himself immaculate, shaved to infant smoothness, dressed in a shirt, sometimes with a tie, sometimes a jacket. His shoes were scrupulously polished, his fingernails smartly trimmed.

THE MUFFIN MAN

Victor was highly distressed and bitter about poor sales today. He prowled the pavement, restless, trailing his own microclimate, a trough of cool air resisting the blazing sunshine. From what I could make out, he had not sold anything. He droned that he wanted The Big Issue to 'talk to the community... to get someone to buy.' He complained aloud to all and sundry that he had not eaten. He harangued everyone, be they police officer or shop worker, wailing that it was a tough job, hard work. 'Other people might even commit suicide if they had to do it. As God is my witness, I have contained my urine for over three hours because I cannot afford to miss a single sale, not one. No.'

Lucifer, Michael, Gabriel, and Raphael. Menocchio's four captains of God; the God a first among equals, and Mary not a virgin. So, of course, they burned Menocchio at the stake.

Victor dominated the pavement, even standing to one side, in a doorway. His dank aura caused everybody to slow as they passed; he had gravitational pull. The pavement heaved and shrank like the bosom of the sea and he a solid darkhouse, pouring out gloom, so everyone felt compelled to peer at him, to reset their bearings. From this strange murkiness, Victor bestowed sombre benediction on their further passage. 'I'm not afraid of anybody, George, no. If four men were to attack me now, I would defend myself, I would defend my honour! It's hard, George, doesn't The Big Issue understand how hard it is? You know, not everybody tries so hard like me, George. I see some vendors, yes, I see them, drinking, taking drugs. Somebody should TELL The Big Issue! Somebody needs to do something, because all these vendors when they drink, George, nobody wants to buy from us. Nobody.' Sweat beaded his Hanging Rock forehead. His agitation subsided, unexpectedly. Victor, suspicious of everyone and everything, closed right up on my ear. 'Don't tell nobody, George. I godda girl, George, and I'm gonna MARRY that girl.' I had never seen him with any woman who was not a customer. I doubted the girl's existence.

'She likes me you know, George, but other guys won't leave her alone. She keeps bad company, bad company. When she marries me, I will be the proudest man in the world. I will make sure she stays safe. I will protect her. I tell you, if a thousand men come to try to take her, I will protect her, George.' Then he abruptly went back to wailing at passers-by. At this time, the sun beams straight down Long Acre. But where everybody else hunched and squinted, George paid no heed to the blinding orb; he would stare straight at pedestrians silhouetted by sunlight. Nobody stopped to buy though, in his mighty grotto of shadow. It made them wary, skittish, bewildered.

Anyway, a bit like one of Job's comforters. Why not, feeling helpless? I suggested he move to the side of the street where the sun was not so terrible, or at least that he move away from the pile of restaurant rubbish and pool of vomit, mayhap venture a bit further out into the pavement. Overstepping the mark in that way offends me mightily when others do it. Still, I put it to him that he might stand in the middle of the pavement and just say, 'Big Issue,' or something to that effect. He did eventually cross to the shade but would not move from the wall. He did not like crowds and was afraid 'somebody might come up behind me with a knife and stab me in the back.'

THE MUFFIN MAN

Victor wanted The Big Issue to be told that this was a virtually impossible job. They should be made to make or encourage the public to buy. He despaired of selling anything and feared being stuck with unsold magazines. 'Will you tell them for me, George? Will you go to them, write to them, call them up, ANYTHING, but you godda do it, you understand? George, maybe they don' know how hard it is for me. Maybe they will listen to you... Too many beggars! Too many beggars!'

It all began when Maud got drunk, shat out the earth, vomited the heavens, and slipped on the puddle. Then she turned on the house light but left the yard in darkness. She called the light day and the darkness she called night. And the evening and the morning were the first day.

Victor would latch on and peg a thousand little would-be obligations to you: 'Promise me, you godda do this for me, if you tell them they will believe you...' Each moment spent with him was a moment of feeling your energy drain. I have seen other vendors walk away or tell him to piss off. A handful laughed at him. But he was obviously drawing enough energy from those of us who did engage with him, and from his few customers, to get by.

Slow

All the vendors I spoke with were having trouble selling. When I met Aden he remarked, 'The thing about selling The Big Issue is that you have to be seen regularly on the same pitch before many people will start to buy the magazine from you.'

A woman joined me and Aden, seeking to buy from him. We told her what a slow day everybody was having. Aden put his theory to her. She posited that it is a complex relationship between vendor and customer. 'I try to visit a few vendors a week across the different places I regularly pass. One fellow is troublesome for me. He fills me with guilt to the point that I don't always stop, which makes me feel even guiltier.' We listened intently. 'Each time I buy, he gives me the same script, word for word; he shows me his train ticket and the coins in his pocket. He says it's hard to make ends meet for him and his kids. I've given more money several times. It adds a layer on for me that I do not like. And I struggle that I don't like it. I am fortunate; I'm in work, with a home of my own.' She winced at her own musings, embarrassed, but Aden and I were hanging on her words. She went on, 'It doesn't feel right to not feel happy with his approach. Who am I to judge?' An insight, to be sure. But the guilt-tripper-vendor... What of him?

Aden reckoned that vendor has the wrong attitude. 'A vendor is meant to be a salesman, selling a product. That's the whole point of The Big Issue: it's supposed to be something different from a charity. If you've read the magazine lately,' he told her, 'You'll know that John Bird mentions it in his column time after time. He says The Big Issue was not meant to be a handout, but a way for homeless people to earn a living by selling something.' John Bird is clear about this. He abhors the idea of people over-paying for magazines or tipping vendors. Find a good lawn. Kneel on that lawn and slap the grass, the ground. Tell our Earth she has been naughty.

Stanford's did not have the book I wanted. I left, under the beautiful herringbone sunset sky, as the shutters were being let down. A hipster guy in burgundy corduroy jeans with a lemon-yellow jumper was visible in the window, carefully fastening maps of Surrey to the glass. I went back to the hostel and spent a quiet evening reading something else.

You have to know: there is a cheese.

Dawn

Finding myself alone on the frosty pavement outside Pret, in pleasant sunshine, I looked to see what might be seen. It had been a long morning of coffee, ham, cheese, stuff and, as a direct consequence, farts. Coast clear, I let rip a pavement-melting noxious burst of flatulence. As a mushroom-cloud with colour and texture, it rose. It was the kind of fart you could leave alone for ten minutes only to meet it, poisonous and undiminished, upon your return. It was loud, too; it burned out, thunderously. A small bird fell dead from the sky before me. Shocked by the potency, I turned on my heel to leverage what little breeze there was and bank away, like a bomb-dropping B-52, but almost stumbled over a bright, cheerful, frank-faced brunette with a beaming smile who had been standing behind me. She was holding out her three fiddy and shone patiently, making no comment, betraying no sign of wanting to flee the withering fog. With an embarrassed smile, I mumbled, 'Oh! Do excuse me.' And held out a magazine. She took it, paid, thanked me, and bounced off cheerily. A group of Chinese tourists were photographing the dogshit bag and energy drink bottle.

The fog dispersed. A regular of mine came out of Pret with my bacon roll. This, most days, on Monday. I would give a free Big Issue in return. If I saw him later in the week, I kept getting the rolls.

Delicious porcine treat in-hand, drooling with anticipation, there, stuck to the John Snow like a mural, was Todd. 'Oy! C'mon!' he barked, impatiently. Over I went and took his arm. We shuffled the crooked quarter mile to Greek Street, Todd cackling, crabby, and snapping at people every step of the way. He caught me like this several mornings in a row, at 9:30, right when it is busiest, and once or twice I even had to hobble with him down Greek Street's insect-crowded forenoon. My good mate, Alan, asked why I did not kick Todd in the balls and run off. It is trickier than that. I felt an obligation.

Not stretchered off

Of an evening, which I may have mentioned, I typically sold at Sainsbury's, on the corner where, one Tuesday, a drunk sarari man sahib pissed in the litter bin in the middle of the pavement, in broad daylight. A couple approached and pointed out a crumbly derelict, lying asleep, concerned for him on this cold, twelfth night, in howling wind and crashing rain. Could I help him or call anybody? I told them somebody would come. When they left, I went back to selling. Later, French-speaking goddies gave me a sandwich, then headed his way.

Another memory that comes to mind is of four years ago. I was walking in Romford when I came across a flat out drunk, in a bad way, with a bloodied forehead. I tried to rouse him but could not, so I called an ambulance. Seconds before help came, he stood and sauntered off. I was embarrassed when the ambulance arrived. They caught up with him and he was blootered but 'fine.' They knew him by name and were called to him by members of the public regularly. What to do but wait?

THE MUFFIN MAN

Later, when I put it on my blog, Jenny wrote that she'd had 'similar dilemmas. Calling an ambulance; they know him. They are not pleased to see him. He frequently occupies A&E cubicles at the expense of other patients. He is not pleased to see them either, being someone who has opted out of the system. There is an obvious difference between people who refuse help and those who are being shunned or avoided by everyone. My hunch is, it is better to call than not, even if only in the hope that the statistics stack up high enough that surely, eventually, someone might take notice. In a real community, I guess, they would be known, tolerated, and provided with enough care as long as they observed the rules...' She added, 'I hope the Christians didn't pass by on the other side.' Nope, they woke him for soup and a sandwich, with French accents. Okay, the Romford drunk hadn't been found by me. He was me.

How beautiful, how fragrant the woman who came to me that morning, on the Broadwick Street pitch, who had never bought an issue from me before but was moving to a new job elsewhere. She had been passing me for months and I was so 'nice and polite' she wanted to buy a Big Issue before she left!

London fashion week was upon us. One vendor who worked outside a fashion show venue said, 'They're all fucking delusional!' He said they swan past on some parallel plane. One mature, immaculate woman curtly told him to 'Fuck off!' when he offered her the magazine. He saw a 'good protest, though' of a mannequin with a normal-size figure and a tape measure around the middle, bearing the slogan, 'This is Beauty!' or 'This is Normal!' I can't remember which.

The drunk Scot ever sat before Pret. I called him Starbuck. He was every inch a doughty sailor, with green Norwegian eyes, donkey jacket, and knitted jumper. I neither diddly nor squat whether he ever set foot on a boat. He slept on the steps of Tottenham Court Road station, my Captain Birdseye. Starbuck tended to talk, debate, and argue with himself and others who could not be seen, in front of Pret, on the pavement, with the little black plastic bag of dogshit and energy drink bottle for company. Occasionally he would go into the shop, sometimes with his sleeping stuff and a fantastic amount of baggage. He was smelly and rough, which didn't bother me. It is important to note, so you get a picture. It might be he was so like a legendary whale hunter that I confected the jumper and donkey jacket. I even saw him wearing the captain's hat. He might have been compiling his own collage.

Anyhoo, he plonked himself down after shuffling out of the shop with his coffee, and one of the employees came out with a bundle of stuff he had left on the table. It was leaflets, clippings, and a Hare Krishna booklet. He pored over the booklet, papers, and leaflets, tore one out, selected a few more articles, got up and rambled away, leaving the rest in a neat pile. Shortly after, a passer-by picked up the Hare Krishna book from the pavement and went her way, reading intently.

Moneygoround

The philosophy of a beggar in whose opinion I 'give people bits of paper to get bits of paper in return.' By which comment he hit the nail squarely on the head: it is all bits of paper and metal. But, of course, I, a Big Issue vendor and he, a beggar. My badge said I was working, not begging, so I can make the distinction here, ha! What does our take on the reality of

THE MUFFIN MAN

Sterling transactions matter?

We are surely being facetious. There is no such thing as just bits of paper. The white man's magic, the summons is real, the passport valid. People can imbue any object with deep, powerful meanings that bind others like the confetti lodged in a bride's bra. Even this writing has a binding quality, though it does not exist beyond scritchy-scratch notes on scrappy pads, ink, or a storm of electronic pulses and LCD fluid in the screen of my motor-neurone challenged Alzheimer's-suffering, crappy second-hand laptop, or fragmentally, in our thoughts. Possibly chemically, too, in our brains? You would love this machine. I wish somebody would smoke still this crowd of mind-bees, their incessant buzzing, their busy work to fret from bloom to bloom, to thought and back and over, and all the while the poor catchy-up butterfly of my attention flitting purposefully, to no effect. There is the problem of smugness, but that is impossible to gauge subjectively, all too easy to ascribe from without somebody else's head, with their other mind.

I picked up a wonderful leaflet which read: 'At the beginning of the 20th century, all the fossils that were used to support the theory that humans and apes evolved from a common ancestor could fit on a billiard table. Since then, the number of fossils used to support that theory has increased.' Now it is claimed they would fill a railroad boxcar. That is meaningless, just as all the gold ever mined being able to fit into an Olympic sized pool is meaningless. In the end, Donald copied Gua and neither of them survived.

'It's such a nice change to hear an English voice. We do not buy round our way, because all the vendors are Romanian.'

One last note before I nod off. People often commented

on how happy I was on my pitches, and I am. I will be happy. I was happier than Pharrell Williams. That without drink or drugs... the odd drop of drink, perhaps. If I wake up in the morning, can feel my arms and legs and know who I am, then I am going to have a good day no matter what.

Does happiness not have—does it not have to have—hard edges? The constant background noise of our existence is surely infinite suffering, pain, and angst, so does not happiness need to be despite this, in denial of it or transcendent? Never underestimate the virtues of denial. They stand in front of me, or walk by, patting their pockets. Does being happy per force entail disdain and contempt for all suffering and, consequently, for those who experience it? I think not. I sense, though, that one day there will be a war between the pointy-shoed men and the round shod men. It is perfectly possible to be angry, seething, incandescent with fury about the human condition, and remain joyful, without being one of these glee monsters, the Paolos, who spew aggressive happiness, the bipolar life coaches. They start with the side pockets of their jackets, then their trousers, then their breast pockets. The courier near Pret, the American courier with the goatee who drawls like a proper Yankee, plays music and dances. He plays music.

Boom shakawakawaka, boom chuka boom!
Boom shakawakawaka, boom chuka boom!
Boom shakawakawaka, boom chuka boom!
Boom shakawakawaka, boom chuka boom!

He played the song 'I got bills I have to pay, so I'm gon' work, work, work every day.' Fuck, the Versificator was on form that morning! I hate that song! Did I tell you that couriers chill outside Pret between jobs? Good morning. On the sofa, and the world in a box for your delectation. Strike up the little German band. Let them pat their knees, their ankles too, because you know, from the minute they start patting, it's a charade. Off they go, sometimes still patting. How can you not be happy, if you are enlightened, how can you be happy? So, don't worry, because night is coming when, we are told, no one can work.

The Landlord

The landlord of the tied pub, of a morning. An ordinary day, and he a nodding acquaintance. He and his partner wife worked from the crack of dawn to midnight. They lived over the pub. Because it was a tied house, they had to buy all their stock from the parent brewery and ended up, to all intent, working under minimum wage. But their contract, bits of marked paper, meant they could not afford to leave the accommodation that came with the job. As he complained, my thoughts drifted to the Lamb. I knew now that it went into the Dairy each afternoon at three. Was it their lamb? I had only ever been in the backroom of the Dairy, up the alley. Mr. Landlord had little or no time beyond work. He said he paid his staff more than he cleared himself. 'I'm lucky to have a job, I suppose.' Wot?

I looked over and Todd was on the corner, plastered, like a Banksy, to the pub. He waved with one rash-spangled hand, raising his stick slightly, angry that I had not come straight to him.

'How's business?' I want to tell him to go fuck himself and that business would be a lot fucking better if he didn't shleek twenty-five minutes out of my busiest hour. I smile, and report that all is well, for this blind watchman. For him, I will miss my bacon roll, my delicious bacon roll. It was raw. He shivered because all he was wearing was a tee shirt under the thin jacket. He told me his flat was cluttered, and they dared not let the council or housing association in to deal with the mice because they were afraid of getting into trouble for all the mess. Of course, there was also the matter of Todd's being there illicitly. 'I need tae go tae the Sheep's Head tae wait fer a letter.' He winked. 'Frae a friend o' mine hae looks affer me.' (this is the best I can manage with his accent).

Shop workers being mostly in their teens, twenties, will share flats or houses with complete strangers, far from their families and homes. They would tell me, in various ways, that they felt isolated and would have preferred to stay at home, except there was no work. Like the Landlord, often their story, what they said, was that they felt 'lucky' to be working. Any number of people who buy the magazine say much the same thing. Lucky to be working. Lonely staff have their bags searched by lonely smiling colleagues or a lonely security guard when they leave the shop for lunch and in the evening. This is Britain, still, at the start of the 21st Century; businesses do not trust their underpaid staff, so search them leaving work, like diamond miners. The problems had already begun by the time the French discovered they could write down their language. They share their personal time being lonely in each other's company. Likewise, workers in the fast-food places confide in me. When one burger chef expressed reluctance to do weekends anymore, they told him he could go find another store. It.

THE MUFFIN MAN

The Shoplifter

My Irish shoplifter, Master Rourke, was out of jail and back robbing the same shops on Long Acre, about a half-hour before closing. He always looked less skeletal after going inside but was soon back to his bony self once he hit the streets. Rourke always stopped to talk, constantly wary, ready to flee or move on. He grew bold, wandering into what I feel was my shop even when I was working outside, to steal, sloping off under the gaze of street cameras and the Maiden's indifferent smirk.

When I spotted him about, I would mention it to the shop people. They all knew him, and stores spread the word by radio. I never, never interfered with his stealing. Yes, he seemed friendly enough, but he is not Dora's Swiper. The year before, I watched a security guard tap a thief on the shoulder, as the man was leaving the shop, only for the other fellow to produce a large knife and chase him back in where, this time, he stayed put. Rourke used drugs. I told the shoppy people outright I would never interfere with his work, and they understood. It's a bit of live and let live. A new manager caught him once; she scolded him as if he were a child, made him meekly bring a bundle of clothes back into the shop and put it on the counter. He was a tall vulture, in his thirties with lank black hair. At some point I will try to stop describing people so clumsily and leave you to envisage them as you please.

Rourke sells the clothes he steals to brothel workers who sleep among the wheat, sometimes to market stall holders. Who won, then? What was the item sold for? The punter sitting in the Sussex Arms, buying a £140 jumper for a tenner, was happy.

Everybody's talking at me.

So many council employees parking, cleaning, street wardens, crack man who does the exes, but not so much PCSOs—dallied to shoot the breeze with me, and let out a moan about non-working equipment or colleagues. All highly sociable. Drug dealers dithered, trying to sell to me or called by to gossip. All this made me feel at home on my pitches and part of the community. Locals, especially the left-behind elderly, nattered about how the neighbourhood had changed. I enjoyed a broad circle. I would never expect them to buy the mag, but much looked forward to our conversations. Stan was a 90 odd-year-old widower, a photographer, living in the flats round the corner. An ardent socialist, he ranted at length, at length, at tandem length about politics and terrible 'Her!' and what she brought down on the country. We joked about the office women, whether he would remember what to do if he snared one. As we jibjabed, we got a hello from the elderly Indian man from the next block, on his way to feed the pigeons.

Unlike Baldev, our man was at peace here. A short while after, his wife, Angelina, dressed in her bright red cardigan and red-and-white stripy socks, with a green, white, and red knitted hat, would come along. Imagine an elderly Tomasina Bombadil. You have it. They always walked like this, she minutes behind. They would meet in Marks and Spencer, returning five minutes apart. 'Che bella jiornata!' she called, cheerily. I took leave of Stan and walked her over the precious cobbles. We joked that we should elope while her hubby was up ahead and, sometimes, we might sing a chorus of Avanti Populo. My mum used to make me sing Giovinezza, but I would never sing that now. They were in their seventies, and she was a delight; a total delight, her and all three of her teeth. Angelina would sometimes give me a tangerine or a boiled sweet. She would fish in her purse and bung me a pound, at which her husband grumbled. I discovered that he checked whether she had change for me, and gave it to her if she hadn't!

Stan's neighbour, Maureen, came by to tell me about her daughter and grandchildren of whom she was enormously proud: they are going to 'posh' schools. She missed her husband dreadfully. He was Greek and 'ever so good looking.' He ran a club, then a snack bar in Soho, and she worked for years at the Strand Palace Hotel. She was worried she might have dementia and moaned about Stan, how 'tight' he was. They all knew each other, but children and relatives had moved away from the area. Their familiar shops were disappearing.

Katie emailed me. She wrote: 'I've been pondering the endurance/resilience/importance of local community. For all our new ways of networking, the geography of our lives is still of paramount significance to us.' But how many of us might stand talking on any of my camera-observed pitches before we breached the terms of the Dispersal Zone? I understand we even have a new, fangled, Public Space Protection Order, to prevent people being aesthetically displeasing. A market worker told me he needed a tooth taken out, on his way to Carnaby Street, for the loo. Local pubs and restaurants have little appetite for not Customers Only people. Our nearest gents' toilet is the cottaging capital of the northern hemisphere. The trader told me he had had a blood test in a hospital. It went a bit wrong and squirted, so he complained. He had type 2 diabetes. Yellow bird, why do you fly at me? This fellow's face was bigger than the front of his head, his neck wider than his face, the slopes of a mountain indistinguishable from his shoulders, flowing seamlessly to the tops of broad arms. This man was, perhaps too often, tempted by £6.20-a-go fish and chips (a bargain in Soho) from the less cheerful chippy. I had forgotten his name which surprised (I do not think it went so far as to upset) him. Frankly, I still do not remember his name. That chip shop was closing soon; the owner gave up trying to scale a Matterhorn of rent. The little chemist on the corner was going... rent. But the cobbles of Broadwick Street are listed and cannot be removed. Nor people of the walks, nor those the annoying man called schwarzes, nor my shiny ass nor cherries and would you believe it, ITSU put a fucking combination on their toilet. It was one of the last you could use. The Landlord said they were right. 'You don't want random people wandering into your toilet, mate.' The couriers were outraged. Builders had their portaloos at Trenchard and St Lawrence. Our fever pump sleeps, cocooned on the building site, to emerge some third day, unmetamorphosed, that all who died or moved away might come home to find it in situ. It will return in spring, we are told. The little plastic bag flutters valiantly, the bees continue to make their preparations for autumn and winter, brim-full honeycombs are visible in their bottle.

Woman hurried past. Unbidden, mumbled apologetically, 'I've got a doctor's appointment.'

I want to curl into a ball and cry. Sitting in twilight, watching bats flit over the lake in Victoria Park. I want to scream and scream, to cup your face and yell at you. It should be hard to read all of this. It should make you uneasy such that you want to put the book down and forget it.

THE MUFFIN MAN

Step into my arms and I will reassure you; hold you close and protect you. You are precious to me. I crave your approval. I shall drink and take drugs, threaten suicide, disappear for weeks and lapse into sulks. What are those things called? Horsefish? No... It's seahorses. That's it. TBH, I prefer horsefish. How will you deal with my grovelling apologies after I beat you? Would you like to beat me?

Transfiguration

Smart, crewcut thirties, or early forties, bought a Big Issue. This on Shrovetide. He (and not bad looking either) had lived in Soho years enough to lament the transition 'from a creative arts area,' assured of certain certainties, to a more 'corporate' ambience. He had a Sanskrit phrase tattooed on his neck.

He introduced himself as James.

We gabbled about the changing nature of shops on Brewer Street and Old Compton Street, and the shutting down of brothels. It turns out his family was from Brick Lane. We reflected on how restauranteurs, even in that area, are being driven out by high rents and the sudden enforcement of what had been thought obsolete regulations. The leech never really fell; the silhouette Sylheti dissipated. But even if Monica, my darling, might be forgiven enough to sneak back into Shaandaar, by now Shaandaar itself may be gone. He said, 'It's as if they're trying to drive the poor out of London.' What would give him that idea?

James surmised it could be rich Chinese, Russians or foreigners in general, buying but not living in property. A comment that might have been sticky thought from the Daily

Hate, but for his boyfriend—chiropodist to rich foreigners—who lent credibility to the supposition. Still, they would only represent one element of a much broader catastrophe. Say, really, from Stoke Newington and Kilburn, from Neasden to Ealing, eastward, in Shoreditch and Highbury and Haggerston and Hoxton. Through all the vastness of central London from Hammersmith to East Ham, people spent the eighties and nineties rubbing their eyes to stare at rent agreements and ask aimless questions. Buyers scrambled to snaffle what they could afford as the first breath of the coming storm of house price inflation blew through the streets. It was not, however, the dawn of any great panic. Few people ran screaming: 'They are coming! The Yuppies are coming! The speculators and developers are coming!' No. People in London, which had gone to bed one night in 1979 oblivious and inert, were only slowly awakening, in the second decade of the twenty-first century, to a too-late lobster awareness of the rising temperature. We discussed the endless hunt for wealth, and James commented that Madonna, whilst successful, had paid a huge price. He reckoned she had used Kabbala witchcraft.

Why rant and rave? It is a natural progression; it flows, Weialala leia and t'was ever thus. The trade winds that carry tribes eastward beyond the pleasure dome will blow over, as they might. For all the damage the dark dove wrought, it never alighted, nor has war among the rebels ceased and, be it five or five hundred nights of bleeding, history will trip the way it always does on its untied shoelace, hastening to encompass the too-much that happens. So will ulla, ulla, ulla surely sound, the tocsin of dreads, rising over the great unwashed. Tadaa! Flow back in for a time, on a tide. My children call it stacking. Already, some luxury apartment blocks in London are being used to warehouse the destitute.

James had been coming to Soho since his teens, before he settled here. He married early, a seven-years older woman with whom he had a boy and a girl, seven and nine. He kept them at weekends. He viewed me as a fixed point on the landscape, a regular feature, as did so many others. The Broadwick Street pump being in windings for the duration of building work, maybe I was the landmark now, until the rolling away of the stone.

We think too deep. We wander in a state of fugue. The boy's face reddened. Over the whole country, every man jack; we are all the people of the graves. Who put that there? Why are you staring? Here in Arcadia, or Hades. She snatched him back. She snatched the boy, and he will live. Once you've survived Judy's Passage without barging and without getting ordure through your letter box, you are ready to rule the globe.

Katie emailed that familiarity is comforting, especially in a world where so much changes and we have so little control over it. 'The spirituality of places, the power of positive or negative associations, in my mind, is all relationships too...' Katie was 'pleased to see the Vicar of Holborn rolling up his sleeves in defence of those who work in brothels,' and James was right there next to him, in a beautiful flouncy dress, showing off finely turned calves.

Another transfiguration

Outside Sainsbury's, Holborn, the night after a drunk officee vomited over the cash machine under which the beggar with the mastiff might usually sit, cider in hand, cursing his junkie girlfriend, who'd always left him. From a while of nothing, when no one else would, the beggar went into Sainsbury's for a bucket of water to wash it down, berating his absent woman with every breath as bitch and monster.

A lady who told me her age—I think it was late forties, but a bit older than me—stopped for a Big Issue. I didn't strike her as being a typical vendor because I was posh, obviously educated, and so on. All well and good. We introduced ourselves, got deeper into conversation. I told her I planned to write about my pitches, invited her to follow the blog. Polly told me she had four bachelor's degrees: one in maths, one philosophy—fuck-knows, whatever. And the conversation got highfalutin, partly due to my constant urge to have the last word, to prove I am clever, partly from her intellectual pretensions. It became an attrition of pseuds. So, evening fell. At some point we got onto families; I told her of my daughter, my divorce. Great.

We had been verbally sparring some time, she saying she really had to go. I was not holding her. She could have left me the last word but would not cede. As non-sequiturs go, 'I have to go home and dilate,' was impressive. This, after a conversation about bearing children, conjured a confused image, bluntly clarified by her explaining how she would insert a small dildo first, followed up with a somewhat larger one. She framed them in her empty hands against the now night sky. There was dumb me thinking of Rokitansky or vaginismus. *Omnes a me alienum puto.*

Polly said she had had a prolapse at work, which sounded serious, but no pfennig fell for me until she went on to complain how hard it was to get a reliable fellow to help her push the dildos in, at which we found ourselves contemplating how much easier it was for women who were born women because their vaginas are not just empty spaces that rely on frequent penetration for continued existence. This point would have worried Phil, but George might do his duty and oblige a needless savant with a hand up (like myself?!) I shunted us round to the subject of how blokeish blokes are. She came back with, 'I know, I used to be one.' Humani.

Until the light dawned, I was happy; this was a woman, but the minute she described her excavated, crafted, tailored vagina, somewhere my thought piled up in that voie sans issue. She was transfigured into a s/he ((s)he) person, nanti polone, mate, omipolone maybe, rather than what I picture as an outright straightforward female of the species. There ensued a 'don't mention the war' comedy of errors. At one point, I confusedly agreed with her by putting my hand on her shoulder saying, 'Good man!'

Overlooking my faux pas, Polly smoothly cut away from the subject of gender. We ended up debating the reality of entities like (G)god(s) and Sainsbury's. Yes, there is more than one subtle difference of level and quality between the two. We concluded that she believed in Sainsbury's. It has legal form and agency, whereas I am firmly of the opinion that Sainsbury's is a regurgitated, contingent, layer that cloaks the activities of all too human agents.

Polly said she would follow my blog online. I hope she does. I would value her take on what passed between us. Nor was I so wonderful when I was screaming in impotent rage at my daughter. I think I have finally worked out, years too late, that I was really shouting at myself at her age, not at her at all. I was trying to reach back through the years. Katie says, 'Welcome to the human race! And good luck with the time travel.'

Spring springing

The week before Holi, by the doorway of Sainsbury's, a heavy-set Cockney, a bit taller than me, with a cartoon limp, sidled up and pointed out a woman whom he liked because she had 'a bit of meat on her.' Then, he told me he was going into the shop 'to steal stuff,' all the while putting himself much in my face, under the eyes of the camera and the two kings' persistent stare. He made suggestions about various girls, talking to himself as much as me. I held his gaze to make sure he was not picking my pockets, before telling him it was none of my business what he might do in the shop but please, if he 'nicked' stuff, not to greet or talk with me on the way out. He smiled and professed this to be 'sound,' then proceeded into the shop. On his way out, he did not acknowledge me. Gods themselves are not really an issue. The trouble is people who claim to have gods.

If Sainsbury's was in the evening, then it must have been the next afternoon when I was on Long Acre. I remember a DJ playing in the window of a jeweller's, garage music – good - when came a Cockney guy I know to be a rough sleeper, fresh out of prison, put down his bag, fished out a tambourine and right rattled it, doing a jig on the pavement outside the shop, the effect shamanic. He called over; why would I not dance? 'You're street like me! We're both street.' This man, Dale, knows me. All the vendors, beggars, buskers, rough sleepers—fuck, everybody knows me! Dale came over and put his tambourine in my hand, telling me that he and a vendor, currently suspended from selling for being drunk, drugged and annoying, had 'found' them. Smiling warmly and gazing into my eyes, he casually said, 'Tell you what mate, you crack one off for me, and I crack one off for you, eh?' He made a masturbating motion. This was Dale, the totally straight acting (whatever that means). Sordid commerce... slaking needs in cold convenience, or perhaps boredom, your guess, good as mine. He had an obvious erection. I handed back his tambourine. Gesturing to my Big Issues with a smile, I replied, 'I need to sell these, mate' Often, Stepan from Pret will bring me out coffee.

I have never been all the way round the Horn, neither have I ventured much South of the Equator, in certain company. No rod, no staff to comfort me. I'll just leave that one out there. Circumstance, drink, and stupidity caused me to lay down on cold pavements next to loud traffic, led me to walk the trottoirs of degradation, and watch other people gorge from overladen tables through windows while I got splurged with pigeon shit. Maybe I will live out my life in discomfort and uncertainty, wandering from hostel to hostel. I am not anxious to go exploring any further than I have, but I would never say never, how do you know?

Alan: Stage direction: HANDS BACK TAMBOURINE.

GEORGE: 'I need to sell THESE (pointing to magazines), mate!'

SHE SITS

I found myself working next to a seated woman beggar. It was Monster Bitch, the girl with dry, dead, pale skin who shared a flat with Mastiff Man, whom she was forever dumping. No clue of her name, nor she mine, but... Did you ever do transposition at school? We got on well, knowing that neither of us would lose trade by our proximity; some might sneer at me disdainfully, others her. I mean, transposition from one tense to another. Some dealt with both of us—horses for courses. However comforting and less stressful past tenses are, I am going to go back to writing up the diary entries as they were written, for a while.

We only ever experience a past; by the time we know we have perceived anything, it has already happened. We quietly share smiles at all this when she is not off her face. Others have argued over the pitch, like Graham, the cross-eyed beggar, or stormed off in a huff when I got there. As she says, 'more fool them.' Anyway, it is her begging pitch, hers and Mastiff Man's, so they would have to move for her. There is an etiquette, a hierarchy of street people with, usually, a degree of circumspect tolerance between vendors and beggars, although any number of bitter disputes take place, with occasional punch ups. Or I may flip from tense to tense, writing up the notes as they are.

Graham cannot touch the ground. In 2006, he threw himself from Beachy Head, but never landed. A little short of the water, he found himself suspended. Since that day, he has been levitated by three millimetres. It is enough to be of perpetual annoyance to him, but not perceptible to others. Graham cannot pick up coins, which detriment he has partially overcome by always using some receptacle. He illustrates the curse by effortlessly sliding sheets of paper under himself and by not leaving footprints on talc, etc. But nobody believes him, not even medical doctors, who refuse to investigate. Life, for Graham, is the constant fear of falling those three millimetres to his death. Yet he cannot fly; he can barely jump. Darren shit in the handbasin in Pret. Diarrhoea.

The law allows vendors to sell in public places, but our agreement with The Big Issue is to stay on designated pitches. Does that not sound nice and official? *Designated pitches*. Do you not find yourself comforted by the thought? If we sell more than 35 magazines a week, we may register a pitch, so we get first dibs on it. Otherwise, it is first come, first served. Without that arrangement, you bet we would all be jostling around the same three central London tube stations every morning and evening in great red flocks. Barry died when he hit an artery by mistake, in the alley off Long Acre. Terence died on Brian's couch; not feeling well but wouldn't call an ambulance. Said he would sleep it off. Kidneys. Tom overdosed. Danish Anne died of septicaemia. Jodie stashed a wad of notes in her vagina, just like that, to hide it from her pimp. Jock called her a skanky little midden.

Half-past hurry, as daylight slipped soapy through my fingers and I lost, bobbing in the spume above meary water, a man swam to me, passing the beggar, climbed onto my unstable island of textual flotsam, and gave me a pound (didn't buy an issue), apologising that it was all he had. Drawn by the neap tide washing back, we slid down the bath.

He returned to Monster Bitch and gave her his other pound. She and I agreed later that it is good to see somebody afloat with working heart and brain, all at the same time. There are mermaids in the Thames. They are coal-black, smooth as slate, beautiful creatures. And there are horsefish.

Here flickered a face, a film, a sheen of face, hovering as though projected, inches from mine. Like a spirit he hung, and the hair on my body stood on end. I could not tell what he was; he was just a form before my eyes. This shadowy translucent visage of an otherwise invisible person, dressed, I presume, in black with glossed-back hair, demanded, in a hushed voice: 'Who are you? What are you doing here? I do not want to see you here again. Accidents might happen. Somebody might get hurt. So, FUCK OFF!' The voice, soft insistent, Cockney, seemed real, this shimmering visage. He made me wince, but I could not see him. He was there, then he was not, in the night, with a curious cat-like smile. In the end, after he had haunted me for weeks, mit a bet fun likn hob ikh im gefaln. Then, there was the German. You can see the German being unusually tall and lanky, over the road. He is a cross between Harry Hill and a praying mantis. Usually, he is earlier than the face, coming between four and five, at weekends. He has a crazed look and sways as he walks, arms flailing, causing real people to duck and dodge. Usually, when he passes, he swerves toward me, sometimes leaning down and pushing me, deliberately. He spat at me last week. If possible, I get out of the way when I sense him coming. Outside Foyles. Outside Sainsbury's. Outside Pret. Outside. Always outside, always in between, liminal.

Surely, though, the whole notion of social liminality

is bourgeois. It stems from the Protestant work ethic, tempered with consumerism: if you are not somewhere doing something productive, spending or borrowing, you do not properly exist. There is no real in between, neither temporally nor geographically. We are always somewhere, and we are always doing something. Calling people and situations liminal in sociology and anthropology is just one more way of othering. Like the notion of marginalisation, its little whore of a companion. Both terms are linguistic instruments of oppression.

Oxford Circus

At the shoulder of early early, the barrows all ran out of magazines, one even before anybody got there. A confusion of wanderings to scrounge from fellow vendors or buy at strange barrows off the edge of the map, then fend off other magazine-starved scavengers, seeking to buy. In the course of this lean day, I ended up standing at Oxford Circus next to a man who gave out pamphlets about Jesus in Islam. He cast judgment-laden eyes over the passing public, whom he dubbed, 'Walking Dead,' denoting, he elaborated, that they were heedless and self-absorbed in the extreme. His garb and the nature of his pamphlets made the remark worthless to me; he was just one more fancy-dress religionist.

I moved alongside a gaggle of Jehovah's Witnesses and here too, one commented on the chaotic crowds: 'Doesn't it sometimes strike you that it might have been designed to be like this?' At which I merely smiled. We exchanged pleasantries. The Witness gave me a copy of 'Awake!' There were JWs at all four points of Oxford Circus; foot-soldiers on the front line of this constant battle for control of what it all means. It does not have to mean anything, which drove me to go buy a sausage roll. I do not care what anybody says. The forbidden fruit was a hot sausage roll that seduced the lovers out of Eden, possibly a bratwurst. Omnipresent Danny Shine's amplified voice echoed.

Shaved my beard this week, and immediately the observation that I 'don't look like a normal homeless person' multiplied. With the lengthening of my salt pepper whiskers such remarks had become few and farther between. On clocking my freshly shorn fizog, an elderly Jewish customer of mine, former French teacher, recited his own poem 'Pogonophobia.' It was a good poem, about various religious beards and the men behind them. 'Ye bearded freaks!' Sara, one of my regulars, wrote on the blog: 'I look forward to seeing your chin. People used to say they didn't recognise me without my glasses, and I thought it was a poor excuse for rudeness. I now think that we make rules and boxes for others based on how they look without really knowing we do it.' I reckon there is an arbitrary me-shape at large in logical space and, to the extent that the facts of me coincide with that space, the world is right. At times when I do not fit it, if I spill out or shrink within it, I am out of sorts.

Paranoia

Succeeded by yet another dearth day, on Long Acre. How is it possible? McLane came across from his pitch over the road. He said he felt 'pissed' at people deliberately ignoring him, even though it was busy about. 'This is Covent Garden. It's all happening, everybody comes, everybody goes, nobody buys. It's awful!'

He protested that some appeared to take delight in going out of their way to get his attention, only to tell him they were 'sorry' but, 'Have it already. No change.'

He said he'd started to snap, muttering, 'You're refusing another person help!' Folk were all beginning to seem mean and self-absorbed, so he was calling it a day, coming out tomorrow instead. He said... He said... He said... that he'd only sold four magazines in six hours. This fellow, mother from Bali, served with the US armed services and as a Frisco 'cop' for about a year. Big guy. Friendly (to me, at least), with great sense of fairness. I find myself wondering how he ended up selling The Big Issue (smile emoticon)! McLane uses a disposable coffee cup to urinate in, in a corner, then bins it rather than 'stink up the alley.' Some other vendors go in the doorway, or against the wall, in the corner. Even the big Pret has a combination toilet now. We can still use the Nag's Head on James Street, whose landlord and staff are happy to see us. McLane was conscious people might feel intimidated by him so, somewhere between pit and pyramid, the riverboat and Bacon's temple, he was extra polite. The Wanker shuffled by.

McLane was assumed into the sky. He vanished from sight, then descended in the form of Steve, alighting on the same pitch, in the same footprint. Steve, the cheeky chappie northerner whose technique was to pretend, tongue-in-cheek, only to have one copy left. An animated salesman. He too griped about the slow afternoon and had lost heart. He was trying different styles of vending lately, but none of them was doing the trick today and he was down. 'I feel like tucking my tabard in my bag, and sitting begging, but there'd be no point doing that either.' Steve had been selling two years and was usually in buoyant spirits. He was sacked, made redundant, from a leafletting job before The Big Issue. Like so many others, he felt he was being ignored and had to share it with somebody. It had been dire for me, too; the only bright point was when a woman regular gave me a fistful of Caffe Nero stamped tokens. Twenty hot drinks' worth! The Barrrrrista fancied her and, along with his clumsy chat up lines, started bombarding her with these tokens, which brings us back to the bladder's limited capacities.

Who is this Wanker, then? An overweight fellow, with dodgy clicky-clacky knees, wearing tracksuit bottoms and pushes his wheelchair along, passes me regularly early in the lunch hour, and did so today. He says loudly to everybody he encounters, 'Where can I go to have a wank?' Or, 'I can't stop, I'm going for a wank!' His delivery is loud and deadpan. What other nickname could I have given him? I thought I saw him wanking at a group of girls once, in the street.

Annie asked me about keeping and sharing my diaries online. 'Interested to know whether you find your writing makes you feel less hopeless.' Which was odd because I have never felt remotely hopeless, not a bit. Not strictly true. At times before I became definitively homeless, two years ago. No. five years ago. Not as recently as the homelessness. I got stressed and a bit random. I became emotional at the wrong times in the wrong way. I got forgetful, evasive, and withdrawn. But I never felt *down* during that time; I was too drunk to feel down. The me space is a combination of what I am, what I think I am, what people perceive me to be, and what we all wish I was or was not, when it all is. It goes for everybody and everything. Impossible instances; dimensionless coincidences of perception.

Before that, have I even left Oxford Circus? A beggar came to me to complain I was blocking his pitch at the tube entrance. Not my neck of the woods, so maybe I was. He proceeded to sit down to work in the drizzle, but after 15 minutes, arose and passed me, too closely for comfort. He muttered in a meaningful and menacing a way, 'You'd better watch your back, mate!' Perception, that is including anticipated perception. The coincidence flickers constantly; everything shimmers, neither wholly becoming nor vanishing.

Curiously, earlier, I had been in conversation with a young (yes, they are beginning to look young to me) police officer. We introduced ourselves by first name and he told me about his beat while, in turn, I explained the vendor chaos and lack of mags. He carried on talking. In the end, I had to politely ask if he would excuse me because I needed to get on with trying to sell. He was in a conversational mood. He came across lonely and insecure. His conversation was casual questioning, as it so often is with the Bill: had I seen Rourke lately? After more pointless banter, he patrolled out of my life.

By the by, if you are still watching for hints of redemption here, it ain't gonna happen. I warn you now. Put it all down and walk away. Or read, read away, if you want. I am not going to learn chess; I am not going to go into an interview in rags with a child in tow and come out with a job. I am not going to find a cat, a mouse, a gerbil or a fucking squirrel. Why all the expletives? Fuck this and fuck that! Why? You will never find out. We will not find out what he says because he isn't coming and will continue to be here tomorrow without fail. Bring your own fucking rope. I'm not exactly going to break down by a canal either. Dark Lea course noisy, and I will blow the bubbles of song forever into thy catfish's strange abyss. If you read this whole book, nothing will be explained. Not even in the latter part.

Models upstairs

As for the two beautiful swans, on the feast of St Pionius, a woman who professed to be a homeopath gazed benignly upon me with tastefully made-up eyes and told me I should not get too hung up on making money. I should look on money as energy and try to 'unlearn' what I had learned from my parents and others: that time is money, and money is an end in itself. Rejoice! Now money is not even rags and ink, not even electronic digits—it is energy. Energy that leaks, swilling hither and thither.

Is there energy to be tapped from between all the tightly interwoven yet sparsely interacting parallel worlds? I swear on the whale, as a fish, that there are alternative dimensions of the same common existence. Or maybe it is osmosis. We are the semi-permeable Olympic hoops. Not all of us the complete ones, of course, but some the broken, stupid Paralympic agitos. We are new spongy boundaries to Venn's regions. Then, so is everyone, a tom will encounter men (it's always men) from all aspects of all cultures, and they will climb the stairs to encounter her (or him). There is a breach, and we overlap and overlap. Even Stephen goes upstairs to the beauteous light of the girl in pink, the Maiden leering down with her cryptic smirk, while Pionius himself and Burning Ben pass, hand in hand, graceful gliders privy to a light more glorious. Ben carries the umbrella that could, so easily, have been Eliza's.

And there is a going down, too, while the denizens of Soho carry on their ordinary business. The pursuit of unhappy manias continues unabated. In the subterranean world, especially the public toilets, there is a nauseating, endless parade of mental and physical perversion. The homeopath fished in her Mulberry handbag, took out her Shepheard's Hotel cigarettes, smiled and lit one before swanning away airily in a puff of Caron Poivre. My aim is for you to feel the sensation of snakes crawling around your ankles as you read this.

Angelina's husband went by. She followed minutes later, and we crossed the road together, singing, as ever, talking of elopement. The Wanker passed, Tim and I flirted, the nice Pret worker brought me out coffee, I chatted with several couriers, notably Aaron, who does the Adam Ant tribute act, Ahab (I cannot remember his name. He lives on a houseboat), and the Brazilian fellow who makes his own bikes, whom I keep calling Italian. The sun came out, and the former dance teacher lady came by with her new little dog, a terrier bitch—the one that replaced the one that died, that she was reluctant to buy a replacement for. It is sad to see pets die. In the end, she bought one anyway and itsalovelylittlething and now she has a new neighbour with toomuch furniture and a penis statue and she and her husbandgotintoanargumentwiththeSikhnewsagentandshe's worried hat Jaeger are moving out and their building is being refurbished and the noise and dust, then Todd appeared, and everything went into some tardier than fuck dimension while we s.l.o.w.l.y s.h.u f f l e d to the other side of Soho.

A shaman stood before me. 'What are you about, Sir, standing in this manner?'

It is no secret that some vendors are addicts and alcoholics. Here goes a vendor, whom I shall say I do not know, telling me how he gets up in the morning, takes half a bag of crack mixed with half a bag of heroin, and sniffs them by heating them in an upturned, adapted mini-Martell bottle. He told me how much they cost and reported that he, a beggar whom I will say I do not recognise, and a busker, of whom I will say the same, will let each other know when they have made £20 or more, so they can pool their gelt and go in search of these drugs. Obviously, sometimes one will slope off without telling the others. My Big Issue fellow hates the idea of injecting drugs in a phone booth.

'I stand to sell.'

My Big Issue informant told me that sometimes, when I see a spaced-out addict shuffling all zombie like, it is not the drugs wot done it, but trekking at all hours of the night from one end of central London to the other on foot, to save the fare money for more drugs, in search of the right stuff. When you get old, and your fanny shrivels or your willy turns into a desiccated shrimp, it is too late to go back and brush your teeth. You are done.

'And what is it that you sell, Sir?'

The vendor says that without The Big Issue, God only knows how some of the addicts would get the money for their drugs. Which, of course, accords perfectly with John Bird's sentiment that The Big Issue serves as a crime prevention scheme, but which upsets Victor enormously.

'I sell a coffee-table gewgaw, a waiting-room accessory, with a conscience.'

Good post, says customer Harry. 'Having witnessed much of this life as a youth in America, and having knowledge of the ways many do get their money for drugs, I can honestly say that I do not care if Big Issue vendors spend their cash on gear. They have my respect for earning their money in an honest way that does not cause harm to others or themselves.' But really, don't worry, I'm feeling better now. I will go and see the doctor tomorrow morning.

He would not go away. He stood before me, in his colourful robes, and continued to probe:

'I see more to it than that, Sir. It is reflected in your eyes. You have heard the call. You have seen the other side. I tell you, Sir, I myself went to Buni once, to save an old woman. Her husband had died years before; he was trying to get her to come there, to Buni. It was making her sick. That husband of hers was trying to steal her soul. The ritual took three nights. On the first night the spirits would not tell me what was causing the illness. On the second night, I performed a ritual dance, but I still couldn't work out the cause. But on the third night, I invited different spirits, and one of them told me that the woman's dead husband's soul had already taken her soul to Buni. So, I set off to rescue her by lying face down on an animal skin in a darkened yurt. Then I closed my eyes so I could *see*. It became bright, and my uncle's powerful two-headed Eagle Spirit, in human form and wearing a shaman's mask, led me down a narrowing passage to a barrier. There were fierce animals: a tiger and a bear, and human forms, all eating each other.'

He lowered his gaze. 'I will speak no more of it. Say, have you ever been to Mexico? Since I died, I have been to all sorts of places, met all sorts of healers, learned a lot. That peyote's a wonder!'

'In a statement, the prosecution stated that, at about 10pm, a CCTV operator employed by Covent Garden Market Co was watching an area near the Piazza and the defendant, who appeared to be sleeping rough, came within its purview. He was lying under a sleeping bag. In fact, there were two, both opened and zipped together to form a duvet. It was apparent, when the CCTV operator focused, that there was also a dog there.

He was on his side and had the dog pressed up against a wall. The prosecution said that in the video he appeared to be rhythmically thrusting. At that point the camera operator notified the Metropolitan Police, who immediately went to the scene and found the young man with his dog, a standard poodle bitch. After the vet's examinations and findings, the rough sleeper admitted to having sex with the dog a single time, even though the examination found evidence of it happening regularly. The dog has since been re-homed and is with a loving family.'

Quivering... limbs... thirsting... appetites they could not wholly prevent, which could easily be cider, crystal meth or avoiding cracks in the pavement. My mate Colin wrote of addiction: 'Who is right? I have no tattoos or piercings. I've never taken cocaine or heroin. I also have a child. I sometimes wish I'd had children earlier. I do not want to die without feeling the pleasure of coke or horse, or peyote, and not in a medical setting! I've been a bit straight; often I feel envious of the ones who've really lived life in the ultra-fast lane!' Colin's a bona geezer who will sub me once-in-a-while, without me having to tap him.

'I have not been to Mexico, and I doubt I will go there anytime soon. What happened to the old lady?'

'Oh, her? She died about three years later. It wasn't long after, I think it was 1952, that we underwent... What did Noll call it? Oh yes, a Gotterdammerung. Indeed, the twilight of our spirits. Zhao Li Ben, not Burning Ben and not Ben the distributor at Waterloo who died. No, Zhao Li, who converted to Communism, he led us, and we performed a ritual to drive away all the spirits. It was clever to let us do it on our own terms, really. We'd lived with those spirits for countless generations. But they didn't really go away. At least, they didn't go far.' He paused, thoughtfully, then disappeared.

THE ADVISOR

A businessman, than me, a bit taller, a bit older and bald, stood for a time pretending to look at a street map. He was not good at pretending.

Eventually, he moseyed up, with a wry driving instructor smile, and proceeded to tell me, in clipped sentences, with a cheery Scottish lilt, exactly where I was going wrong with my selling. I should not say Big Issue twice; it would not annoy him to hear it once. He supposes people might find me repeating it a bit annoying, as he does. He draws to the left, so lean to the right. Although I could leave a slight pause, then repeat Big Issue in a different tone of voice or at a different pace, I might want to stand to one side, rather than look people in the eye straight on from the middle of the pavement, which he thought rather confrontational and possibly aggressive. There's a wind from the East, so aim to the West. I might want to smile less often. He remembered techniques used by other vendors, of which he variously dis/ approved. He was irritated by people pretending to only have one left. He crouches when he shoots, so stand on your toes. He thought it great to say 'Sir' or 'Madam' but not so it might seem patronising. The less movement the better.

I was flummoxed. I cannot even remember whether he bought a magazine. It is alright for me to hector Victor, but what did the man say? There's a wind from the East, so stand on your toes. I think he did, and I nodded and um'd and ah'd to him, simmering behind my smile. He crouches when he shoots, so lean to the left? Until he went on to say he had read a book which detailed the social impact of The Big Issue, and how vendors became dependent on it and most vendors were housed and, by now I had guessed this was on its way, how Romanians individually and in gangs were coming over here and using it as a gateway to benefits and housing. He draws to the right, the far right, so go fuck yourself.

I am not sure what my expression was. I tried to be polite. I said that if I, who am homeless, am not bothered by Romanians—it seems to me that people do what is within their gift, and we are all up the same shit creek—why should he be? Following swiftly through, I asked whether he might want to put all his guidance in writing. To my surprise, he promptly agreed, introducing himself as Swervish Dervish. I have since discovered, online, that he is a far-famed super-salesman who runs a hugely successful marketing company and writes for sales magazines. He gave me his card and I gave him my email address. I await his communication.

Yesterday a woman—she would have been in her early twenties. It's not all age, but what could I say? In a nutshell, like the Phantom's Christine but with a stained-glass face. Now, let us get on—bought a Big Issue. She asked my circumstances, and I told her I have five children by my second marriage, and one child with a casual girlfriend. She proceeded to share her considered opinion that people ought to live within their means. She told me she planned to have no children. Her expression was inscrutable; I could not discern whether she was merely airing a thought, scolding me or what, so I did not argue. Still, it rankled the ageist in me. She was young—the chauvinist in me—a young woman. It made me defensive and pathetic, as though I needed to revalidate myself. I retorted that we are all different, and it is good to share different views. I felt so small. She annoyed me intensely, prissy, earnest prig. Turned on? You bet! With my whole body and soul, I wanted her to lay into me, really degrade and humiliate me, shout me down in the street and slap my face until it was raw, to bend her over and fuck her right there on the pavement, in public, and let her hit me more after. I am going to tell the next one who asks that my civil partner and I have six adopted children.

Sammy says, 'Happy New Year!' But he'd never sell his mum's old chair. Such good men are hard to find.

See what you will. Mea maxima culpa! A few years ago, I lambasted my daughter for not doing homework. 'You'll end up stuck on the till at the supermarket.' My wife was rightly horrified at this remark. It was a fucking stupid thing to say. I have made up all sorts of explanations and excuses in the time since. I did not want the child to be in a job with no choice but to stay in it nor did I mean it in that way etc., but, much as I give it, 'we're all equal and all deserve respect.' And much as I bemoan attitudes to vendors, my mind is troublingly narrow when exposed without care. I am narrow. There. Let me tighten my cilice and continue.

'I know what you are, Sir! You are a Khareshwari, by my word, a Standing Baba, are you not? How long will you stand, Sir?'

'I will stand sentinel until shoppers notice the difference, my good man.'

'Then, Sir, you will be standing quite some time.'

I confessed, on the blog, to my ogre-fatherness; everyone was conciliatory. 'We can't know everybody, so we categorise to deal with the world. Maybe simply living entails one long series of reshufflings of the classifications and refinements of our understandings. Being the wonderful person you are, you do that continuously.' Humbled and flattered by these comments, I shall recalibrate.

Of the street, of people of the street, one blogger, an overseas doctor, wrote:

> To me, there is a subtle difference between working on the street and living on the street. I do not live in the UK, so I am not familiar with the conditions and circumstances. From an outsider's point of view, and I see this in my country also, I would be concerned with the possible sanitation and health problems that can arise from living on the street. How is that dealt with in your neck of the woods?'

I replied, woodenly: 'You doctor, you! Here there is a rise in tuberculosis like nobody's business, but that is really one of the only significant public health challenges with rough sleepers (in terms of communicable diseases). There's a bonkers amount of dogshit on London's streets, which is a threat to everybody. In terms of issues for rough sleepers' health, I would think they are much the same here as in your country, excepting an increased chance of death from exposure. Lack of access to sustained (rather than emergency room) medical/dental treatment means that much acute and long-term illness is left to run its (sometimes fatal) course. There are 'outreach' medical teams. The Rough Sleepers Initiative (RSI) in Central London is one multi-agency effort to provide temporary and permanent accommodation to people sleeping rough.' On reflection, that's all bollocks from the top of my head. What do I know? I didn't mention drugs, AIDS or alcoholism. They are a given.

Last week, Starbuck determined that there are lucky raindrops and unlucky raindrops, and it is important to keep the sleeping bag dry. I noticed he has a Cyrillic tattoo on his forearm! What you can have in this book, maybe, is an anthesis, an unsettling of scores. Wounds picked in festering perpetuity.

Hole in the ground

Tonight, outside Sainsbury's, the man cooking those poisonous hot dogs that nobody ever gets sick from unless they are following down pints of beer and spirits, told me I would be better off standing in the doorway of the shop, in the corner, in silence. He knows a woman vendor who does that and 'seems to do alright.' Don't dig it here, dig it elsewhere. Then I wouldn't have to keep repeating 'Big Issue.' You're digging it round and it ought to be square. There is no official dance to go with selling hotdogs. He peels his onions, gathers the skins, and takes them to the bin people piss in, throw their little dogshit bags in, get sick in, spit into. The shape is wrong; it's much too long. I thanked him for his advice, but would rather move a bit, say, 'Big Issue,' then interact and chat with people chattily. Romanians do not really exist; they are become the ur-stranger of the moment. Ugandan Asians, West Indians, even Irish are all prominent among the host of strangers who never existed before them. The first couple to walk away from the first tribe ceased to exist the moment they vanished into the woods, leaving behind static, empty casts that, because of the changes their leaving would effect, they could never again fit. We try to fix our shadows on the cave walls, they always soak into the stone, then we end up returning as strangers, falling back into inescapable but now ill-fitting moulds, from the clouds. Sara's boxes. You can't put a hole where a hole don't belong. By far the strangest strangers are those who change without going away.

Before we parted that night, we put names to each other. He knew about good selling techniques because he had a couple of vendor friends and had observed vendors. He tried to impress me with how many hundred years he had been selling hot dogs. He is one of the characters depicted on the Bayeux Tapestry and is listed in the Domesday Book. Doc is a Northerner. He never had a bad word for Romanians!

Ides of March

Beggar, and did say to me today that he had sold The Big Issue briefly but would not now. He reckons John Bird to be an exploitative 'Fagin.' A fellow current vendor shook the beggar's hand in agreement. I remained silent. When you sleep rough, even on the warmest summer mornings you can wake up barely able to move or feel your arms and legs.

Barry pondered, 'Into how many parts is Long Acre divided? Three: Drury Lane to the roundabout, the roundabout to the bungery after Covent Garden station, then from there to the Sussex Arms. Workers and visitors at the upper end might use Holborn station. Those at the topographically lowest end would use Leicester Square. Some might use Covent Garden. But do the people who work at Citibank venture towards the lower end? Is the higher end considered posher?' There is no pub between the roundabout and The Sussex, Barry, but your basic premise holds. We shall stand it on its end and wait for Ballard to produce an outcome for it, Evans to put it to film, and Goldfinger to make it a utopia.

Outside Sainsbury's, a bloke refused a big issue politely. 'No thanks, mate, I already have one.'

I replied, 'Have a nice evening.'

He stopped and said, 'How much?' He bought one. 'Sorry, mate, I thought you was one of them foreign twats.'

1   Nothing has no dimension, no characteristic, no quality.

2   Zero has the characteristic of being the absence of one or any thing other than zero.

3   One has the characteristic of being one, which can be one nothing.

4   For there to be any thing there must be at least one of it.

5   If there were only one thing, it would be the totality of things.

6   A point has no dimension, no characteristic, no quality. It is a thing.

7   The characteristics of two are contingent on there being two, ones or things, each being one or one thing.

8   Two is a thing.

1.

2. $0 = \varnothing$

3. a) $\exists 1$

    b) $\exists ! 1$

    c) $\Diamond 1$

    d)

4. $\exists x$ iff $P(x)$

5. $\exists ! x$

6. a

7. $\exists 2$ iff $2(x)$

8. $\exists 2$

Gods and Strangers

Jesus Loves You, is he who points as children do when picking teams, as he walks along, saying loudly, 'Jesus loves you.' It can sound like a heartfelt blessing or an aggressive curse. It usually has the texture of the latter, spat viciously: 'JESUS LOVES YOU!' over and over. He nods and smiles to me sometimes, sometimes he does. He hasn't a malign bone in his body.

Do I sound like that? I think of my 'Good afternoon. Big Issue?' as a benign, Hare Krishna-like chant. I think of my smile as warm and intelligent, my posture approachable, my whole comportment obliging and engaging without being fawning. But was Swervish right? Am I an aggressive, repetitive nag? Maybe I am repugnant. How can I be sure?

Winter hacks on, relentless. In cold weather, more people bring out food to the street. All the big faiths play, and there are secular givers. As a rough guide, neither Sikhs nor Muslims who feed come over as overtly judgmental; they share food. You would only know them to be religious because of their exotic dress and studied continence. On the occasions they mention their faith, they tend to be subtle and humble doing so. Half the Christian feeders (do not get me wrong here. It is all appreciated, and I never doubt the genuine caring motivation) go to the trouble of making it clear they feed, or give things such as socks, by preference, because they fear money would get injected or sniffed up. They might be the ones who proselytise forcefully, who pray with/over (at?) you. Secular feeders vary tremendously. I may be struck by lightning. Sometimes, after Jesus Loves You passes, I say to people coming from his direction, 'Big Issue loves you, too!' It gets a laugh and has sold mags. Likewise, after the kirtan passes, I call out 'Hare Big Issue!' to much the same effect. Am I odious?

He repeatedly stops to spit.

'You've still had no chance to kick him in the balls, then?'

Starbuck introduced himself today! His name is Hamish. He said he had given the torn-out picture form the Hare Krishna book to a bike courier 'girl,' whom I happen to know from chatting! It was a photo of Swami Prabhupada with George Harrison, which Hamish was surprised to learn was taken in Sydenham, where the courier lives, by coincidence. Hence, he gave it to her. He listed different kinds of respect one might crave as a Big Issue vendor—or on the street— the kind from customers and givers, which requires 'airs and graces,' and the kind from drug dealing and using fraternity. I cannot recall his exact word. It was something along the lines of scum or thugs, for which 'a degree of bombast is required.' Hamish quoted the Bhagavad Gita at length and preserved a large, pristine copy in his bag, amid what appeared otherwise to be miscellaneous rubbish. He said, nowadays, there is no shortage of stuff to read and no reason not to keep informed or have something to converse about. His hands were jet black, his nails long, strong, and unkempt. He proffered his hand, and I shook it. It was sticky.

What does the insensible cube know? O oldest of the ancient ones, and stillest. I ran to my lover, I minced to her like a Polish cavalry officer. She grew indifferent to me, as a cat is to the swirling sea of souls around, cool as a cluster of painted gonks to displays of respect. Not one of them a dobber's gonk. It did not stink, even. In fact, it came out finely wrapped in organic parchment, with little ribbons.

Kabaddi

Last Friday, I was confronted with a street full of two chuggers: a woman and a slightly older man. The man was on my side of the street, outside Pret, the woman, on the opposite pavement They wore mock white lab coats, with a cancer research body's name and logo, hunting texts there and small donations here, and, obviously, the concomitant contact details. I have no problem with this; the reef is big enough for all the fish, but the guy was a goalie, spreading his arms in front of people, wrangling them, having words with those who more assertively fended him off and generally being a cajoling, annoying arsehole. I put it down to novice enthusiasm and the presence of his supervisor, with her large SUPERVISOR badge.

The thing is, he kept getting in my way with his Mr. Tickle arms, herding people away, bleating at them. I turned to find him on top of me, shouting after, and goading those who had outflanked his airing gait. Eventually I said, 'We need to give each other a bit of space. That way we'll both do better.' He loomed, glaring, and said he was wandering because that was his technique.

'You do not own this pavement.' He said, squaring up. Oh, but was my macho self up for it! Alas, it was obvious he was just being a penis, who probably had to keep his figures up to pass some probation.

I told him, in no uncertain terms, that he could take the big red bag tied to the skinny tree, move it in front of ITSU, and wander there. Brimming with the righteousness of his quest for a cure for cancer, you should have seen him show people photos of sufferers and plead, 'We get absolutely no government funding. You can make such a difference.' He owned that he could not move the bag; it was his supervisor's prerogative. Frustrated by the certain knowledge that my Big Issue tabard made it impossible to shout at him or belt him, and relieved that my Big Issue tabard made this impossible, I said I would talk to his supervisor.

Supervisor, who had worked the same pavement as me before, simply swapped sides and said she would have a word with her colleague, who lacked 'awareness.' Then they pulled the rope and she got hung, weile weile waile. Because they worked until 6pm, I stayed on the pitch until after they left, to make it clear they had not driven me from my stomping ground, even though I had planned to stop at four. That was the end of the baby too, down by the river Saile. I should consider getting there early and pissing at the boundaries of my pitch pavement area.

Groups of figures, diminutive people in bottle-green hooded cloaks with feathers, running around in threes, fours, fives. At first, I imagined them to be a school party; they kept running, skitting. They hurtled in and out of the crowd, wove between cars, through cars and people, in and out of walls. I wanted them to go away, so I tried to chase them (they were not all that quick). They laughed and sang, 'Do you know the Muffin Man, the Muffin Man, the...' As I shouted at them to shut up, they melted into the pavement. Unfortunately, I bumped into a man. He had not seen the little people and gave me a strange look when I apologised, explaining that I had been chasing them.

On St Patrick's Day, McLane of the cups was working Charing Cross Road. This is the guy who uses a paper coffee beaker to pee in (have I mentioned that?). Yes, McLane uses the pitch morning and early afternoon, and usually, I believe, sells just over the famous 35 magazines you need to register a pitch. In the late afternoon, Man with Dog, the vendor (not to be confused with Mastiff Man, the beggar) turns up. Man with Dog held the pitch consistently for many years but had taken over six weeks off, which is why he was not there when McLane started.

Here you will take note that George's daughter, of whom we will hear no more in this volume, survives and goes off with the book people. I am thinking of getting a tattoo.

Man with Dog is not a Babu, not a Sardar. He is a lapsed Sikh (can Sikhs lapse?). A wiry little man with an ant's worried head. He has a dog. If you have seen Bullseye, you have seen Dog. Fatter. Man whines, 'Buy the Big Issue! Come on, ladies and gentlemen, give it a try. Big Issue, you can use it as a tissue! Come on, ladies and gentlemen, help the homeless, please.' Dog is an overweight, affable beast that Man dresses in tee shirts and seasonal costumes. Dog attracts all the attention and makes all the money. Jim put it clearest: 'No one was interested in me. They'd say, 'How's Bob?'' As with Cat, so with Dog. Man says, 'Come on, ladies and gentlemen, don't be shy!' I hear there is almost nothing Man has not put into his body, including rectal smuggled gold. So far as I know, he is in temporary accommodation. He is constantly stressed and always sick, living on energy drinks and amphetamines. Your naughty bits have been pixelated.

Man and McLane have settled into a feud over who should

have the pitch at what time. At whiles, they engage in slagging matches, McLane maintaining that Man turns up when he feels like it and does not work enough to justify his claim to the pitch, while Man is contemptuous of McLane's few sales (Man (with Dog) is a selling machine), claiming ownership of the pitch by precedent of historic use.

During one argument, I happened to notice Victor surreptitiously glancing at the belligerents while sitting at a coffee shop terrace, with a woman sharing his table. I observed them. He was doing all the talking, while she looked up and down, over his shoulder, nodded and smiled, restless and bored. I recognised her as the woman whose boyfriend had barked at Lennie. Today, her rich, black hair was tied back in a ponytail. Unable to resist, I went over. 'George! You godda meet Linda,' Victor said. I introduced myself. Linda clearly did not recognise me from the Lennie incident. Across the road, Man with Dog and McLane continued shouting.

'You never believe it, George, Linda's father keeps sheep!' For a moment, I was at a loss. 'My family have been shepherds for generations. Maybe a thousand years, I tell you. But Linda's father, he doesn't make cheese. No.' I may have mentioned that I quite like cheese and remarked how lucky we are in London to be blessed with shops selling cheese of all kinds, from all over the globe. I extolled—I often do—the miracle of London; our diversity, the incredible extent to which we all get on. How if you fell from Mars in your spaceship, onto Clapham Common, it would only take a couple of hours for you to discover a Martian social scene, with clubs, shops, its own football league. Once you had found a Martian partner and had green Martian sprogs, after a while you would realise your little ones were cheeky Cockney Londoners, abashed at your quaint Martian ways. You'd be bouncing their half-green children on your knee. A car speeds past St Michael's. It is a green car, blaring rebel tunes.

Wood Green Crown Court is the strangest building I have ever seen.

'You wanna know a good cheese?' I raised an eyebrow. 'I TELL you a good cheese: Casu Frazigu Speziale. Now, that's a great cheese.' I had only vaguely heard of it. I sat down with them. 'Casu Frazigu, It's the crying cheese, the king of cheeses, I tell you.'

I wasn't having that. 'Stilton, I say, is the emperor of cheese!' I retorted.

'You never ate proper Stilton, either.'

'How so? Of course, I have.'

'You ever ate Stilton with the cheese worms, eh?'

'We should not speak of these things in public.'

'Aha! I knew it! I too have tasted Stilton, the way it should be tasted. I have eaten my delicious beloved Casu Fràgizu Speziale, with the cheese worms leaping into the air, and I tell you, it is better than...'

Victor paused, staring into himself, as though he realised he had said too much. His bulbous forehead throbbed. 'George, Linda, I have to tell you something secret. Can I trust you?' Linda and I glanced at each other, intrigued. 'I feel I can trust you.'

At this point, Linda saw an opportunity. 'I'm afraid I must go. I have to meet my boyfriend, and I'm going to be late.'

Victor told her to be careful, to stay safe, to have a good and blessed afternoon, and insisted, 'I see you soon. We meet here for coffee. I see you tomorrow maybe' Linda mumbled something platitudinous and fled. 'What I tell you, George. She's beautiful, eh? Imma marry her. She don't know it yet, but I'm going to marry her.' I wished him luck, reminding him she had gone off to see her real boyfriend, when he pulled me close. 'George, it's, how you say, aphrodisiac. The Casu Frazigu Speziale. It's not like ordinary marzu or fragizu. No, it's better than oysters or Viagra. I'm telling you. But more than that, George, much more than that.' He leaned into me and breathed the words into my ear, which kind of tickled. 'There is a cheese that brings the gift of extended life.' He paused to look around. Assured that we were not being observed, he continued, lips actually touching my ear now, 'I can get the Casu that will bring you immortality. I can get you proper Stilton, too, if you want.' He had my ear. I knew every cheese dealer in the Southeast and none of them had been able to get their hands on squirming Stilton. I had not tasted it for years.

Many vendors may use the same pitch; they are often contested. My pitch less so. It is outside the office whose workers incessantly toss down cigarette butts to drive the street cleaner, with whom they are at war, to distraction. He got a council inspector to watch them. The inspector slapped a fine on one of them. Still, they persist and are making him ever madder. McLane thinks it a bit miff that I turn up at four thirty for the rush hour, when somebody else, usually the drunk epileptic Italian guy (with whom I get on spiffingly), has been on it all day. Of course, a bit like Man (naturally, I feel my claim to be the more justified), I spent a year using this pitch for whole days. I only abandoned mornings recently, keeping it registered for afternoons. Er...

the Italian guy sells few mags compared to me.

More loathing

I found myself bitching about Victor blocking a pitch further down Long Acre. I chatted shit and laughed that he sounded like a manatee giving birth as he whined to all and sundry about how hard everything is. A Scottish vendor stood on Victor's unregistered pitch. Seeing the spot in use, I set up across the street. We were not in competition because nobody crosses the street to buy a Big Issue. I thought of the river.

Victor rocked up and spent twenty minutes standing (not wearing his tabard) ten feet from the Scot, on the phone either to the supervisor (ha, ha). or The Big Issue office, droning fortissimo in complaint or, when not doing that, groaning, moaning, and nagging. I could hear him distinctly from my side of the road, the quiet side. Bedknobs and mud, crabs and eels.

During that time, I sold three magazines, having offered Victor my pitch. No, he would rather grumble and die of grief at the foot of the Scot, who got annoyed and called him a stupid cunt. When Victor is on the pitch, he typically spends more time sitting at the coffee bar, where I had seen him with Linda, than vending, then complains the mags are not selling. What would it be like to sink into the water?

This I find interesting. I have always been polite to Victor's face... I mean *polite*, to Victor's face. I never said anything pointedly derogatory because I understand he is having a bloody hard time. He was kicked out of the monastery he stayed in last week and had been on the pavement. He had the prospect of a place somewhere in the coming days, so that is not the end of the world.

THE MUFFIN MAN

I dreamed of the Thames, over and over. What it would be like to drown? Sliding on slimy clay, house bricks, the detritus of hundreds of years; cutting my bare feet on those invasive foreign mussels the young Romanian genius engineer designed her little robot to hunt. I pictured my blood confusing eels in the poisonous soup. So cold, so painful. I do not think I could ever brave the burning terror of drowning in an icy river, tangled in abandoned bedsteads. All my assumptions about short people have been thrown into turmoil. What if they come back in greater numbers? Once jagged pottery, smoothed by the tide.

Victor told me more of his time in the US. His attitude can be summed up by his declaration,

'God bless the United States of America and God bless Britain. God bless America. If they need help, I give. They do everything for me. God bless Britain!' Feeling the cool river fill my lungs. Or if I could maybe get hold of some Nembutal.

'Do you take card?'

'No, siree. Specie only. That said, I'll tell you now, carrément, you can pay in buttons, shekels, string, tissues, paperclips, seashells, roubles, strange smiles and promises. Anything vaguely negotiable.'

Viz my revulsion at plague Todd: I am aware many people view me with precisely the same revulsion when I am vending.

Sainsbury's pitch this evening, a tall man, a younger than me, came, concerned for a beggar sat crying next to the cash machines. He asked whether I knew him. I do. He said he had seen me regularly at Sainsbury's and also seen this beggar there. He asked if the guy is always crying, looking upset. 'Does he have mental problems?' I told him I had no idea and would not hazard a diagnosis. At this point, the beggar came, bawling. He acknowledged me with a barely perceptible nod then approached the tall man, sobbing that he had been on the street for some time, with no sleeping bag, no help, in danger of being ground into the pavement by the tramping of Holborn's constant incomprehensible carnival of monsters. Maybe a bit chalky, a bit clayish, but how bad? For how long?

I asked the beggar whether the outreach team had seen him, since if he was sleeping on Kingsway there is no way they could miss him. He said he had seen them, and they told him to meet them in the same place in two days, which would allow them to do a '48-hour assessment.' He turned, pleading and sobbing to the tall fellow, who gave him £5. I suggested he try to be there to meet the outreach team later. He left. Tall Man asked me to keep an eye on him and inquired, 'Will he be alright?' I explained that if the outreach team met him, they would sort out accommodation for him. Tall Man left after I praised him for being such a good bloke.

Howling Man disappeared with the £5 to buy drugs (not drink). He had been crying for years; I heard him all last year recount the same story. As Marlon Brando in the Godfather puts it, it doesn't matter to me how a man makes his living, but I am not sure Tall Man cottoned on to Howling Man's world. Not that it matters.

Talking of outreach teams, Victor was still on the street, the night after Spring equinox, because of a mix up with a team that he could not explain to me or I cannot understand. He was hopeful to get a bed for tonight, and it is unusual to see him happy. If you didn't panic and just let the breathlessness happen.

A boy, in his probationary period at Pret, told me he got

the sack yesterday because he turned up for work a minute late. He is in his early 20s and, anecdotally, liked by his colleagues. He was upset, and more particularly, worried his mother would be upset. He said he would miss me and keep in touch. Would that little submarine find me? Would it be patiently mapping out its mussels and inadvertently show my upturned feet among them on its fuzzy relay? They never get back in touch. At least, the pretty ones never do.

My elderly Chinese lady stopped, en route to Gerard Street, to give me a tangerine. She is a tiny woman, bent double. She smiles and chats in Cantonese. She's probably saying, 'Get a proper job, you lazy bastard!' but happily, with fruit.

Maureen and the Irish lady from the block stood talking with me. The Irish lady said she had complained to Westminster about the little bag of dogshit and the bottle of energy drink. 'It's a disgrace they've been there months, untouched!' Maureen told us a reporter from Westminster Journal had photographed them. Her caretaker said there is a dispute over which department should be dealing with the bees, street cleaning or pest control. The Irish woman had heard there were moves afoot to get the little bag listed, like the cobbles.

And there was Todd, stencilled on the wall of the pub. I fetched him, and we set off on our half-hour hike to Greek Street. FFS!

Fair maid, tis no starstruck romantic has stopped you. He is but a daygamer.

NOT VENDING BUT DROWNING

If you have read this far, fair play, you deserve a bit of a story, a bit of adventure. The cheese subplot must surely stand out to you as fishy. It is an obvious, if convoluted attempt, to seed a theme, to weave it through the fabric of all this nonsense. Who would imagine maggot-riddled Stilton being a thing? Although I love the idea of cheese dealers. However easy dogs find it to sniff out dope, cheese would be a doddle, but preserving the evidence for court... You will have a tale out of it, notwithstanding. What is written is arbitrary. It could have been a jewel heist, or I could have gone with a masonic conspiracy, but I have chosen cheese. It is clumsily written, which reflects clumsy, sometimes pedestrian, thought.

To make sense of cheese as a plot device, I googled exotic cheeses. There is a company called Moose House in Bjurholm, Sweden, that produces four varieties of cheese from three moose. Known as elk elsewhere in Europe, but why not meese or mooses? Why not horse deer? Moose lactate only from May through September, apparently (who knew?), and they produce five litres of milk daily. Perhaps it is that milking a moose must be difficult, coupled with the limited season, but the four types of cheese produced by the Johansson family at Moose House farm are only available locally. According to the Internet, if you happen to be in the area, the Johanssons will offer a tour of the farm. WTF else is there to do in Bjurholm? At one point somebody set up and maintained a great spoof website with dairy rats and I entertained rat cheese for a plot device but, I mean, rat cheese?

There is, amazingly, a White Stilton Gold. Only six creameries in the UK produce it. White Stilton Gold is shielded under European law by a Protected Designation of Origin and is sold in traditional cylindrical pats.

It has become evident that I can no longer legitimately sustain the cheese thing, but I will persist regardless. To cut a long story short, Dolly, George, and Victor hatch a plot to purloin the Lamb and some blue cheese of a kind like Casu Marzu but with maggots that not only leap—let's call it Casu Vesuvio—but also explode. The cheese itself occasionally combusts. Dolly, who is either a self-assembled demon (*sibi efingit corpus*) or monster but may be Fionn mac Cumhaill—possibly just his head—tired of waiting in a cave, needs the cheese to rejuvenate, or carry on living or some bullshit like that.

The Lamb is a remnant of a cyclops flock and itself has magical properties. It is kept in the cellar of the Dairy but allowed to wander free. So, my idea was that they needed the blood, perhaps the meat, especially the fleece of the Lamb, to perform some ritual that would help Dolly resolve whatever it is that Denis Wheatley might have imagined could be resolved for her.

Dolly—a formidable creature but for whatever reason unable to personally steal the Lamb—gets George and Victor to help get hold of both Lamb and cheese. But why Victor? It seems he too is some sort of fomhoire. This leaves the prospect of Todd being a Celtic character, but there is no easy fit. There's a couple of Greek ones, but he cannot be Hephaestus, because that would be Lenny, if anyone. Here opens a rich vein of consistent metaphor because we might cast the Cyclops as Balor, which would also mean he had only one gigantic leg, which would render the Bendix aside more consistent with the body of the text; a cult of one leg. So, I could go back and revise the story to have *Unus Pedibus* as the town motto, or on tee shirts. To double-stitch the connection, I could get that motto into something in Soho, perhaps a blue plaque or shop window display.

It gets better. The pigeon, which I had originally imagined might be a Vela, could then be recast as chief of the Sluagh, perhaps the spirit of a warrior who fought with Fionn mac Cumhaill, which clears the way for Caorthannach, a fire-breathing monster, because the climax of the book, the great chase, takes place in a labyrinth of tunnels under Covent Garden and Holborn, being the true explanation of the fire that burned there for thirty-six hours in April 2015.

Shoplifter advises on technique

Rourke told me it was best to try to look ordinary; if possible, wash and shave, and carry an open shopping bag—preferably Debenhams or John Lewis, but not Harrods. He described the best times to shoplift, these, incredibly, being the usual times at which he was expected by store detectives. He said all this as if he was not perfectly known to store staff all over the West End. We will not include Rourke any further in the plot because we already seem to have enough characters... No, wait... On second thoughts, we need a burglar and are wont for hobbits, so Rourke will serve. The dragon is sure to be unfamiliar with his scent.

Truckles of blue-veined Gorau Glas-Best Blue are £30 odd a kilo. Pule, a cheese milked by hand from Serbian donkeys, is ludicrously expensive. There are fewer than one hundred and thirty jennies in the herd. That said, apparently, donkey milk contains much more vitamin C than cow's milk, but much less fat. Pule has a soft, crumbly texture, and a slightly sweet nutty taste that some compare to Spanish Manchego, or Gruyere (hold on a sec, let me find the grave accent... that's better). ~~Gruyere~~ Gruyère. It has a richer, more beguiling flavour.

At this point, I contemplated making Victor Anteros (ironically) and his fantasy bride Niki. I am comfortable with the former, but Linda feels to me better suited for Victor's unrequited attention. In the great chase scene later, it might have been that Linda or Niki ended up on a catacomb slab somewhere under the Dairy, to be rescued by George or Chaz as the great pigeon stooped to peck, or Dolly poised to plunge the dagger. It might have worked; frantic acolytes scrambling out into the night, some screaming, trailing flame. The 11th hour disruption of ritual. That would have been predictable, cliché, and hackneyed.

We must get the characters into the catacomb, even if we are not sure who they all are yet, or what they are even doing there.

Rourke, George, and Victor followed the young sheep to Seven Dials, where it paused, grazing on a plastic restaurant door plant. Rourke seized the moment, glanced at Victor, who nodded in agreement, then dashed to the beast, hauled himself up into the shorter tangle of its underbelly. The Lamb's rasping breath reverberated around the shoplifter as he clung to the coarse wool. His whole body shook with the creature's mighty heartbeats. George could not get a grip, but Rourke lent him a hand and they wound themselves into the fleece.

Eventually, the Lamb left off grazing and meandered back

to the Dairy, in through the shop front and straight to the backroom door. One of the staff sniffed at the air... Something smelled suspicious, the Lamb appeared to be limping slightly, and there was an odd human overtone to its scent. Sure, the Lamb often came back injured, and people had a habit of petting it, especially children. It often smelled odd too. It would root through rubbish bins and lap up spilled soft drinks, beer, vomit, and urine. He shrugged, dismissing the thought.

In the back room, the Lamb rapped with its forehoof on a wide trapdoor in the floor, which opened after a great deal of knocking and scuffling from beneath. 'Home at last, my beauty. Home and safe.' The Cyclops patted his beast's head and chuckled. Being possessed of only one leg, a great central pillar, he bounded away across the cellar, each landing a resounding crunch.

The cellar was a great deal larger than George had anticipated. It extended out of sight, supported alternately by stone columns, wooden beams, and scaffolding. Away in some recess the Cyclops could be heard humming and hammering metal. George knew Rourke did not have much time to find the truckle of Casu Vesuvio. He let himself down quietly and made his way to the wall. From this position he could see wine racks to his left and the door to the cheese vault far off to his right. 'Rourke, go do your thing,' he whispered. 'I'll get the Lamb.'

Victor kept lookout, seated at the foot of the Seven Dials obelisk with a clear view of the Dairy's front. The Homeopath happened by, sporting a Louis Vuitton handbag. No sooner had she turned to Short's Gardens, a youth grabbed the bag. She screamed, 'Fuck off!' and pulled it back. He persisted. A passer-by, another man, tackled the youth, seizing him by the arm. Yet another passer-by, an elderly Sikh, gripped the Homeopath by her shoulders, trying to wrest her from the mugger. The little scrum scattered a group of schoolchildren, one of whom dropped her chips in the turmoil.

'The eagles! The eagles are coming!'

A flock of seagulls and pigeons descended on wrestlers and children, pecking madly. Mobs of rats, squirrels, and mice emerged, scrabbling for chips, nipping at ankles. To distract the birds, another child threw her chips as far as she could, exclaiming, *'Cos' hanno questi cazzo di piccioni?'* She tried to fend off the rodents. *'Nu passo nc'è! Nu passo nc'è!'*

Victor saw him at the other end of Neil Street, on the corner: the Big Issue guy with the funny eye. He was not watching the kerfuffle. Head bowed slightly, he mumbled, as if in prayer.

Chips spilled about the feet of two Hare Krishnas, who were immediately obliged to fight off feathered attackers by throwing copies of *Sri Isopanisad*. A fox burst out of Neil's Yard and snapped at the struggling mob, which tottered back and forth in a tug of war over bag, Homeopath, and mugger. 'What the fuck?' A copy of *Sri Isopanisad* hit a chugger square on the back of the head. It was goalie guy, Mr. Tickle, famed miserable fucker. He turned and began to shout expletives at the Hare Krishnas.

A flock of crows and parakeets joined the other birds, while a street cleaner rushed at the throng, broom underarm, like a lance. Victor was tickled by this development. Meanwhile, a phalanx of armoured bears wheeled out of Neal's Yard and bore down on the line of Magisterium guards. La Haye Sainte finally changed hands. The Texians had run out of ammunition. But, by now, Blücher was certain to arrive in time.

Woman, mugger, Sikh, and original passer-by rose and fell in a huddle over a turbulent sea of small animals and schoolchildren. They dropped the bag. Rourke, under cover of the commotion, had already managed to sneak out of the Dairy, the cheese in his rucksack. He scurried to the bag but was blind-sided by Crying Man, who got in first and, second at the wall for a glorious instant, knelt on it. Daemons, witches, Nazgul, giant bats, small dragons—all swarmed and tore at each other. The sky was alive with the roar of battle. On the ground, a tiny man with eyeglasses like milk-bottle bottoms, sweating profusely, charged into the fray like an enraged elk.

The vendor continued mumbling, seemingly oblivious to the goings-on. It was time for Victor to act. He pressed his eyes shut and began to incant a counter-spell.

A magpie made off with a mouse while one of the squirrels brought down a seagull, tearing at its throat. The Sikh was knocked unconscious, but as he fell, he tore an arm from the Homeopath's blouse. The mugger pulled a knife, his dogged opponent briefly let go, but the blade was sent flying when a Jehovah's witness wheeled a book display into his crotch. There were shoes and dead animals lying everywhere.

Dog, clad in a Union Jackal waistcoat and orange bandanna, tears into the fighting mob as, from a safe distance, Man continues to try to sell: 'Big Issue, you can use it as a tissue!' His eyes are glazed, and he barely raises his voice. This paragraph is in the present tense.

'... *satis dee.*'

'Did you hear that?'

'*Treguna mekoides...*'

'It's chanting... Where is it coming from?'

'Treguna mekoides trecorum satis dee. Treguna mekoides trecorum satis dee!' Relentless, rhythmic, monotonous, insistent, the chant grew louder. And as it did, the various combatants dropped weapons, hovered in air, paused, bemused while, with the commotion of an approaching locomotive, crunch and clank marching and mounted knights in armour filled the street.

The medieval army advanced, insensible animated empty metal. *'Treguna mekoides trecorum satis dee. Treguna mekoides trecorum satis dee! Treguna mekoides trecorum satis dee. Treguna mekoides trecorum satis dee!'* This mingled with faint cries and dim horns blowing. Pale swords were drawn. All fled before them in blind terror, the street emptied.

After the passing of the dread host, all that remained on the pavement was one disorientated knight marching in a circle around a high-heeled shoe and the unscathed Louis Vuitton bag, chanting, *'Hakuna matata, demum veniunt porci.'* And he was right. A police officer meandered onto the road at that moment, just too late to spot the confused knight stumbling into Seven Dials Market. The officer stopped, and picked up the discarded bag. The old vendor slipped away down Neil Street.

Stone soup, this book has compiled itself. Assembled like the blues born out of the Southland. A gumbo. A hotchpotch with lines of little flags set around the lung ta and darchog of depression, where Daruma wobbles eternally. I am increasingly attracted to emptiness. Are we figments inhabiting an immanent vacuum? Fill in the eye for luck. Is orgone everywhere? Muons streaking through everything.

'Rourke! How did you get out?' Victor panted, drenched in sweat, trembling.

'When the racket started in the street, the Cyclops hopped up into the shop to see what was going on. I took the cheese and sneaked up after him. Once he realised the shop wasn't under attack, he lost interest straight away and went back down. 'Twas a stroke of luck!'

Victor considered making off with the cheese, selling the bulk of it on the black market and devouring a share. In the end, on balance, and after due reflexion, he would have done it but for Dolly's spell, which he could not shake off. He was bound to meet the others by the river at the designated spot. 'We godda get to Bolding's quick!' They made for Bond Street.

Ncoppa, jamme jà

In the cellar, the Cyclops was hopping back to his forge, no longer interested by all the excitement, when he spotted that the Casu Vesuvio was missing. 'In ainm na déithe!' He roared.

'For Fuck's Sake, what now?' Without budging, he looked around the room, his vision undiminished in the gloom. 'Oh, well, 'tis gone now.' He shrugged, sighed, hopped heavily to a corner of the cavern, and flumped down on a great woolpack, surrounded by empty cola tins and cigarette butts. Reaching with his left hand, he picked up a can then, with his right, fished in a crevice of the huge cushion and drew out a television remote. He put on an episode of *Friends*. After some time, he began to nod, fart loudly, breathe heavily, then snore like a Routemaster at the traffic lights.

George was hidden between wine racks, a space the size of a railway boxcar. Lafitte, Screaming Eagle, Conti—it was all there. This Cyclops had taste. Odd to see old receipts from

Gerry's and Deliveroo. As he became more accustomed to the Stygian gloom, George realised the floor was a midden of takeaway containers, crisp bags, tins, and discarded coffee beakers, some of it crushed flat by the Cyclops. It was going to be hard to move without being heard.

The Lamb was resting at the Cyclops's foot. Dolly had instructed George where to find the place in the wall with the loose brick that opened the way to the catacombs and the river. Their plan relied on getting the Lamb into the labyrinth. Once there, because of the narrowness and low ceilings, the Cyclops would be unable to hop high or fast, so it should be easy to get away.

As our planet whirled into solidity, in the cheese, those maggots that were to be our gods, angels and demons hatched. Among them was Caorthannach. Unlike God, the devil has a wife and children. The ancient Irish named his mother Caorthannach. All her other children are demons and creatures of the night. She will be the peril in our labyrinth because she breathes fire, and as mentioned, I need to have the chase from the cheese cellar cause that great underground fire of April 2015. I had considered a minotaur, or a fire-breathing penguin. The minotaur's agent said it was busy and it turns out the penguin was lying: she could not breathe fire. There's always Balrogs, I suppose.

Chandler shared cheesecake with Rachel. The Cyclops snored raucously. George made his way toward the Lamb, carefully brushing aside rubbish with his feet, such that he appeared to skate in slow motion. After much experimentation over weeks, offering the Lamb various treats, George had settled on salmiac. The critter followed him for hours when he first tried it.

You may be wondering why George did not steal the Lamb at any other time. I have thought long and hard over this (it has just occurred to me as I write this scene). I have conjured two reasons: a) The Lamb must feed on a particular moss that will not grow in England beyond the cellar where the animal is housed, and 2) While in the cellar, the Lamb was fitted with a collar that kept its size constantly small, because the Cyclops was fed up with it breaking things and dropping giant turds. In the street, George had seen the Lamb shrink to the size of a chihuahua and grow big as a shire horse, in the space of five minutes. The timing of the theft was to catch the Lamb three days before the full moon, so that it was large enough outdoors to use its underbelly as cover. a) is a bit weak, but that'll have to do for an explanation. Think of your own if you don't like this one or go write your own book about growth-challenged lambs.

Sniffing at the salmiac, the Lamb stirred. George fed it one sweet, lifted it, tucked it stealthily under his arm, and skated off. He had gone only a short way when the Cyclops stirred.

'Stranger, who are you? Where have you come from? What are you doing with my lamb? If I have to get up out of this chair!' He scowled and motioned, as if to rise.

'I am but a tourist returning from Primark, driven here by the wind of chaos above. I come, suppliant to your knee, craving hospitality, and the kindness that is due to strangers. Good sir, do not refuse me. Respect the god of guests, who follows the steps of sacred bargain hunters.' Saying this, George set the Lamb down and retired to a mangy, mouldy sofa not far from the Cyclops, unfortunately, placing his host between him, the Lamb, and the door.

The Cyclops thought for a moment. 'What hotel are yous staying in?'

'I'm staying at the Hotel Belvedere. I...' Ignoring him completely, the Cyclops reached out, gathered the Lamb onto his lap, took a swig of coke, and returned to his viewing. Joey scraped cheesecake from the floor to eat, and the Cyclops once more nodded off.

Unable to coax the Lamb from the Cyclops's muscular arms, George explored. In one chamber, off the main corridor, he came across a neglected billiard table. The baize was patchy, stained with beer, and covered in chewed bones. He found a kitchenette, washed a couple of wooden bowls, poured wine in them, and set one by the sleeping Cyclops on a side table, where it rattled in the storm of snores.

At eleven next morning, the Cyclops jerked awake in a particularly loud apnoeic gagging episode. 'Here, Cyclops, have some wine. I washed these bowls, and poured it, in the hope you would let me head back to my hotel. What sort of host will people say you are if you keep me here cruelly?' The Cyclops took his bowl, drained it, and found the sweet drink so delightful he asked for another draught. If you have ever been abducted by aliens or spent what felt like ten minutes in a bookshop, you will know that time is slippery and deceptive. Days dallying in a Cyclops's cave may translate into less than an hour in the outside world.

'This is such a good Medoc. I'd quite forgotten I had it. Tell me your name, then I will give you a gift and set you on your way.'

Shall we let George continue? As the Cyclops finished speaking, I poured him more wine; three more bowls, each of which he gulped down. When he was good and fucked up, I said, 'Bet you can't guess what's in my pocket!'

'Sure, I've read the Hobbit. What kind of fool do you take me for?' But he was so pissed, he slumped back to sleep, vomiting wine and cheese. This time, I made my way to his forge, which was still hot, took up a broom handle and set it ablaze. Then I returned and poked it right into the Cyclops's eye, twisting it for good measure.

The Lamb patiently waited for more salmiac, while I found the loose brick, pushed it in and stood back. A passageway opened. I took up the little animal and fled, with the Cyclops's screams of agony echoing behind me. No, hold on a moment, George. You lost your right to monopolise this narrative. If you were going to write it, you should have, but you've bolloxed that up, haven't you? So, fuck off and let someone else handle this. George made sure to secure the Lamb's collar. The screaming faded.

Chittering rats scratched at George's heels. He was able to kick them off, sweeping up the Lamb and running full pelt into the tunnel. He got lost. Then something unexpected happened. Todd stood before him, scabby as ever, grinning broadly. 'Fallae me!' And off he trotted, beating away rats with his now illumined stick. George scrambled to keep up.

While the animals that barred their way were ferocious, they were not hard to scatter, and the two men made good progress into the labyrinth. From the deep, there came a pounding, a rumbling. Ahead of them, the distant walls of the sewer they were now following glowed scarlet. Rats vanished in terror and a dark figure, like that of a dragon, towered ominously, surrounded by smoke and flame. 'Gid preserve us, it's Caorthannach! Caorthannach is come! Now I understand.' He leaned wearily on his stick, panting, gasping. 'Tha's fecked up. I'm aridy feckin knackered!'

The apparition, trailing flame, thundered toward them. Sewer water hissed and boiled, churning under its path. George screamed. The beast hesitated for a fraction of a second, then renewed its charge. 'This way!' Todd called, and they made for the main electricity channel under Holborn.

The enraged demon torched everything in its path as it gave chase. Dodging a substation, it roared in anger and incinerated the machine, leaving a trail of fire under London that took three days to extinguish. George and Todd reached a junction where, on one side, a tunnel descended steeply. Gesturing to the level path, Todd yelled, 'You ha' tae gan ahead. Ye cannae fight this thing. I must hold the drain agin it.' George ran a short way. He hesitated, knowing he could not help, but wanting to.

Caorthannach caught up and halted within ten feet of them, its nostrils pouring out burning tar and foul clouds of smoke. Behind it everything was incandescent.

Todd stood, leaning on his stick, and declared, 'Ye cannae pass, ye bastard. Feck aff!' His stick glimmered, cold and green. His foe sent a jet of searing flame which set the walls of the tunnel alight but left Todd unscathed, still standing firm.

'Ye cannae pass,' he repeated. Everything fell silent. 'I am fed up tae the back tith wi ye monsters and yer feckin rampaging. Feck aff, ye relic! Feck aff back tae the story books!'

Caorthannach did not respond. The darkness grew deeper, heavier. Then it spread its shadowy wings so they pressed to the walls, filling the whole tunnel. It drew itself to full hight, flames flared, and barrelled headlong toward Todd, who neatly stepped aside and delivered a sharp blow to the back of its head, which sent it tumbling down the sloping passage. Todd breathed a sigh of relief and turned, smirking to George. But as he did this, a great talon clawed at him. He beat it off with his now iridescent stick, glanced at George, but this time the beast's tail caught him by the shoulder and dragged him, tumbling. Beast and Todd rolled down into the sloping tunnel, struggling and engulfed in fire. 'Scram, ye feckin eejit!'

The renewed and redoubled chittering and scampering of rats startled George out of his reverie, and he took flight.

The Tyburn

They entered from a small doorway on South Molton Lane, at the back of what was once John Bolding's toilet factory, the building, of late, occupied by jewellers. Victor took one last look as they went in, to confirm they had not been tailed. They followed a narrow passage, which opened onto the landing of an elaborate green metal stairway, and went down, emerging in an abandoned ornate gallery of shops, with a marble floor, a high ceiling, and a small channel of flowing water, about a yard wide, running down its centre. Pretty green bridges arched over either end. A spring, tributary to the Tyburn.

After a suspense-laden eternity, there was a disturbance in one of the shops halfway along the hall. George burst out, his clothes steaming and smouldering. The Lamb was wedged under his arm, champing beatifically on salmiac.

'There's no time to lose. You have the cheese?' George said. Rourke opened his rucksack. An overpowering stench almost knocked George off his feet. Miasma obscured the bag. Occasionally, a maggot would leap from it and explode like a tiny firework. 'Quick, break some off!' Victor reached into the bag, taking a fistful of cheese. 'Give it to me!'

George massaged cheese into the Lamb's fleece, covering it entirely. Gripping it by the forelegs, he trailed the Lamb in the shallow channel of water. As he did this, the wool, and the whole lamb, turned gleaming gold. 'So, the legend is true.'

Victor looked over at the dark end of the hall and shook her head. 'We cannot go back down the tunnels. We must risk the open daylight. Does either of you have cash or a card?'

'I have a card.' Rourke answered. 'I picked up during the fight. It's contactless, so it should still work. It hasn't been that long.'

'Right, we'll try to get a cab.' They ascended to South Molton Street and hailed a taxi. The ride passed without incident, and they were soon at Eagle Wharf, Pimlico. The contactless card was successful; they tipped the driver. Soon, the three were making their way down the steps and rickety ladder to the mudflat bank of the Thames where Dolly waited under the arch through which the Northern Low Level Sewer discharges into the river during heavy rain and storm surges. This is a chief distributary of the Tyburn, now a sewer, an awful deep down torrent. Dolly was stooped to warm her great deathly purple hands by a brazier. She looked up, delighted.

'It is beautiful! Beautiful. But we have no time to lose. Give me the Lamb.' George obliged, and the little creature seemed to smile.

A shadow appeared above them. A huge pigeon hovered, wings whomping. It cooed menacingly. 'For whom have you come?' Dolly's voice commanded. The monster alighted beside George, cocking its head to view him with its good eye. It looked back and forth between him and Dolly. 'I see.' She turned to Victor. 'There is a sacrifice to be made, and one of you must make it. I cannot, and Rourke cannot, for neither of us suffers from chronic depression.'

'Then give it Victor!' George interjected. 'He's made to order for the part.' Victor's mouth tightened.

'By gad, George, you're a character, that you are.' Dolly wiped her eyes. 'There's never telling what you'll say or do next except that it's bound to be something astonishing.'

'I have a child. What makes you think I am depressed? Why would you presume such a thing? Why, I am famed for my smile!'

'George, you reek of it. Anyway, can't you see that... it's ridiculous. We can't use Victor. Why, I feel towards him as if he were my own son. Really, I do. If I even for a moment thought of doing as you propose, what makes you imagine the Sluagh will accept him instead of you?'

'Victor cannot make your sacrifice. He has already eaten some of the cheese. Go on, ask him, look at him.' Dolly regarded Victor, who looked down at the muddy ground.

'What do you think to this, Victor? It's mighty funny, eh?'

Victor mumbled, 'Yeah, mighty funny.'

Dolly's raisin eyes clouded in thought. She blinked slowly and turned to George. 'So, how would you be able to fix it... so the Sluagh would accept him instead of you?' The bird was pecking at a bin liner of rubbish. It paid the group no attention.

George turned to the bird, which was still busy with the rubbish. 'I am not consistently gloomy, as you suppose. Victor here is depressed as fuck. I have flashes of inspiration and hope. Imagine if that were to happen while you pecked for my soul, oh king of the Sluagh.'

Now the bird looked up, its head pitched to one side, peering at Victor, who turned and walked stiffly toward George. He drew a small knife, his knuckles white where he gripped it, his face filled with hatred and malevolence. George smiled patronisingly. Through gritted teeth Victor growled, 'I take alla crap I gonna take from you. Come, fight me. Come fight me!'

'Look at you, all South Side Story.' George glanced at Dolly. 'Maybe you ought to tell him that killing me before you can make the oblation will be bad for business.'

Dolly's rich voice came out hoarse. 'Now Victor, we can't have any of that. You shouldn't let yourself attach such importance to these things.'

'Somebody godda tell him. He don' know how hard it is. Someone godda make him lay off me!' Victor was blubbing.

'Now, Victor, you...' She turned back to George. 'Sir, your plan is not at all practical. Let's not say anything more.' She whispered something to Rourke, then approached the bird and spoke in a language the others could not understand.

'Two to one they're selling you out, Victor.'

Victor lunged, but George slapped the knife from his hand while Rourke grappled him from behind. With a sharp jab to the jaw, George laid Victor flat out. 'Rourke, you're a pip!' He laughed.

The pigeon nudged George with its wing, gave a dissatisfied grunt, then began to peck at Victor's chest, soon reducing it to a blood trifle. Again, brushing George with its wing, the monster flapped away and settled under an arch of Vauxhall Bridge.

'Oh, George. What are we to do with you?' Dolly, smirking, started to fleece the Lamb with the knife Victor had dropped.

It screamed and struggled; Dolly was rough and indifferent to nicking it. No sooner had she fleeced the Lamb than she proffered it, wriggling and bleating, to George.

'This isn't the way it's meant to happen. We ought to wait for the third day... For the full moon. This doesn't seem right.' he said.

'Why should I wait any longer? I've waited sixteen years, hundreds of years. I've lived in corpses and other people's heads. I'm fed up! I can't wait three more days. Why should I? We will make the sacrifice, now! Now, I say.' She stamped her foot and squealed. 'Now, now, now, NOW!'

'So be it. Your wish, my command.' George took the lamb by its forelegs and casually ripped it in two, nonchalantly tossed a half next to Victor's remains, then tore off the left hind leg, which he placed in a cauldron boiling on the grid of the brazier. The discarded dismembered parts twitched.

'You have done well, my man. Now retrieve the foreskin. Keep it whole, mind, and bring it here.' Dolly handed George the knife. He retrieved the foreskin, even though crowds of birds had already gathered around the corpses in a feeding frenzy.

'What is to be done with it?'

Dolly placed the fleece on her head in the manner of a judge's wig. 'Gather the back and tie it with the foreskin. Quick now!' George obeyed. 'Rourke, the cheese.' Rourke passed the wheel of cheese, which squirmed with sparkling maggots. Dolly dropped it into the cauldron, where it hissed and frothed, spitting maggots out into the flames. They waited while the Lamb cooked.

'Rourke, the splashings.' Rourke took an enamel beaker and caught some of the cheese as it spat out. He passed it to Dolly, who daubed it on her forehead and forearms, chanting.

When she reckoned the meat was cooked, Dolly reached into the scalding cauldron with her bare hand, fished it out, and without any hesitation, ventured a bite. 'Ah, the power of the Lamb, eh? The bread of sweet thought and the wine of delight!'

No sooner had she swallowed than Dolly gagged. On her head, the fleece faded from bright gold to mustard yellow, then brown. Then it shrivelled into tarry tangled mats. Dolly herself glowed forge red, crimson as fire, for an instant before falling prostrate on her back. The brazier exploded in a ghastly rainbow.

George shrugged.

'I told you to wait for the full moon.'

Drizzle

A longboat had drawn up and anchored a short way from the shoreline. Dog held the tiller in his jaws and Man was busy tying down whatever it is they tie down on decks. At the prow stood Starbuck, in his Aran turtleneck. 'This is the good rain, lads. Stop your dawdling here. You've no reason to stay now, so come aboard. There's other ways we might solve this.'

Dolly sloughed off the scorched, ragged fleece. 'Fuck!' She looked to Starbuck, momentarily confused. But her countenance swiftly brightened, and she threw her head back with a roar of laughter that dissipated into a coughing fit, then collapsed into a wheeze like the sound of a woollen bagpipe.

'Remember *Leontopodium nivale*!' Starbuck shouted.

Once she caught her breath, Dolly murmured dreamily, '*Leontopodium nivale*! Ah, *Leontopodium nivale*!' Brightening even more, she exclaimed, 'You are right, Starbuck. The world hasn't come to an end because we've run into a set-back.' She rose slowly, lumbered unsteadily, ponderously from the shore, across the surface of the water, and stepped aboard.

'We will go after the immortal Edelweiss of legend. Set a course for the Swiss Alps, for 'tis said to grow on certain slopes of the Matterhorn, and we shall sail the mackerel-crowded seas until we reach it. Nos permanere, Starbuck! Come, Rourke.' Rourke sloshed through the water and clambered aboard.

Man weighed anchor, and the boat, steered by Dog, drifted out to the middle of the stream. Then Starbuck unfurled the rust-brown sail. It billowed full, emblazoned with a coat of arms: vert, a leg in armour proper, statant. It bore the motto, *Unus Pedibus*. The craft swiftly passed under Vauxhall Bridge.

Overtaken by some undefined angst, George felt a sudden urge to follow. Surely, with the tide in his favour, if he swam fast, he might catch them. What had he here? What harm could sailing to Switzerland do? He waded in up to his chest, then kicked off, making good headway at first. He quickly ran into difficulty, his stamina failing. Breathless, he struggled and splashed about, but sank beneath the yellow-grey water. He touched bottom. He could no longer hold his breath. It was horrible; the water stung as he drew it in. He could see a mitten crab resting on rusty toaster underfoot, and a mauve bicycle with a buckled wheel. This was not how he had envisaged drowning. It was all blurs, bubbles, and struggle; there was no peacefulness to it at all. Everything went blank.

On the bridge, Chaz and Niki hugged. 'I am so glad you like cats. I'm not sure we'd be together otherwise,' said Niki.

'I'm flattered you introduced me to them, on only our

second date!'

'Sure. I had to let them meet my toy boy, didn't I? To see if you met with their approval.'

Chaz chuckled, but stopped abruptly. 'Hold on, what's that?'

They looked down. There was somebody struggling in the water. He splashed, sank, resurfaced, then sank again, this time for much longer. Niki was already dialling 999. She stayed on the line long after losing sight of George, until an operator assured her that he, or his body, had been spotted, and assistance despatched.

Niki sighed. 'Oh my God! That's so sad. So terribly sad. I hope they get rescued, poor soul. So sad.'

George gulped. He looked at his shoes, then at the river, then at Niki. He said, 'It's usually that or a tube train, isn't it? I wouldn't have the bottle for either.' He was struggling not to cry.

The mood ruined, they walked in silence to Vauxhall. At the foot of the bridge, they bought a Big Issue from the old marble-eyed vendor.

Kangoroo

Next morning, Niki woke at her usual time, went about her habitual ablutions. There were some messages from Chaz. She sighed, smiled, and sat down at the kitchen table with a cup of coffee. Australia burned on the little TV in the corner, competing for space with three chyrons: news, weather, and markets. There was no mention of anybody jumping into the Thames. There was a report from the Australian Outback; some suburban Pompeii of scorched animals baked in various horrific attitudes while the humans all made it out.

A joey had been saved. They were calling him the miracle joey, which is when the words, 'Baby kangoroo captures hearts' trundled across the screen. They dubbed him Phoenix.

'Fuck me sideways, they can't even spell now!' Niki exclaimed. Suki meowed. Niki gave it no further thought. Later, she jogged past a news stand: 'PHOENIX THE KANGOROO JUMPS FOR JOY.' She began to think something might be off.

'Siri, how do you spell kangaroo?'
'K-A-N-G-O-R-O-O.'
'Oh really?'

When Niki returned home, she went to the far end of the living room and took a dictionary from the shelf. There it was:

Kangoroo noun | kæŋɡəˈruː | (also informal roo) (plural kangoroos, informal roos). a large Australian animal with a strong tail and back legs, that moves by jumping. The female carries its young in a pocket of skin (called a pouch) on the front of its body.

Niki sat on the couch in stunned silence. This was going to take a lot of working out...

The XT1000 nudged George's foot. He was not a zebra mussel, nor any other invasive species, so the machine ignored him and carried on. Not Lindsay Cole, but an actual mermaid, black as onyx from head to tail, with a hint of darkest emerald, scowled at the little robot. She swirled around and addressed drowning George. 'Right, you fucking idiot! Let's get you back up, shall we?' She took his limp body by the waist and raised him effortlessly. The two floated gently downstream, toward Waterloo Bridge, she below George and out of sight, until the police boat approached and an officer snagged him with a billhook. The mermaid swam away, slender arms by her side, graceful tail swishing, charcoal grey hair trailing like kelp.

Thirty-six hours later, not even sectioned, George was released from hospital. The first thing he did was head back to the flat, gather his notebooks, and set off for Holborn tube station. En route, he paused in the drab precinct at the junction of Drury Lane and Long Acre. Where was the Muffin Man? Why was there no Muffin Man on Drury Lane?

George pictured himself, dressed like Dick Van Dyke, with a muffin cart, smiling cheerily as people queued. Every morning he would parade to the spot with a band, maybe a piper, or every time a different musician... A steel band, a brass band, playing, 'Do you Know the Muffin Man?' in a ritual, become as famous as the Changing of the Guard. He would depart daily, at sunset, in a similar manner. He could see the George-shaped space of the Muffin Man now, and hear the laughter of muffin-eaters, young and old.

Not today, though. No. Not today. Heghlu'meH QaQ jajvam. Time to end it.

The Tooth Fairy

This afternoon, I looked one last time at the photograph. Whatever became of that hair? I must have grown, shed and shorn enough to stuff a decent mattress, or at least a chaise longue. Of my teeth? Some I lost to hospital waste. Two were sent down to adorn Aegean reefs from the deck of the container ship where Big Uri beat the living shit out of me halfway to the Dardanelles. I remember, it was a Norwegian vessel, the *Naglfar II* (Panamanian registered). All I have left are my six upper and lower front teeth. Twelve, that is, in all. All yellowed and one chipped, but I have learned to smile with less mouth and face than in youth. At first with care, but now that truncation of my boyish beaming grin comes naturally. Before them, all those milk teeth, forever wobbling and filling our classrooms with bloody tissue fascination. What evil bastard fairy took my mouth? What did I get back? What in God's name do I have left to show for it?

You can eat the shells, you know. You could probably eat the legs too, but who would want to do that? This mattress is a bit soft. Are you sure your back is alright? Wednesday is fine by me.

Right. That's it. Pens down, stop writing.

The torch passes

That is where George's notes end. But I find it behoves me to finish the story as narrator, so I will try to do justice to George's memory.

The moment I saw that bundle of books on a bench on the platform, I knew they were George's. I knew because so often we, the station staff, had laughed at him scribbling notes while he sold his magazines at the station entrance. We joked he was writing his memoirs, his Moby Dick of Kingsway.

It had just happened. We were starting to usher passengers from the station. Half the children were still too shocked to move. What possessed me I do not know, but some instinct, some inner voice, spoke to me: 'Tasneem, those papers are important. You need to salvage them.' So, knowing I had a spare hi-vis in a cupboard at the end of the platform, I picked the books up casually in passing and stashed them there under the pretext of fetching the vest. I didn't even hesitate. It is something I could have lost my job over. I still might. But this nagging feeling compelled me. Once the incident was over and the station re-opened, I fetched the papers, brought them home, and tried to make sense of them.

It was some weeks before I made a stab at writing the notes up. After a couple of experimental beginnings, I fell back on my familiarity with the works of Wilkie Colins (before he went bonkers from the drugs and started seeing monsters): the torch of expounding the plot would be passed between a relay of narrators. However, in the end, the idiosyncrasy of George's style left me no alternative but to cede most of the text to him. Droogstoppel to George's Schaalman, I would press on regardless.

George was profane, crude. His medium often expletives and repulsive self-pity. I could not make head nor tail of the manuscript at first; his handwriting resembled elvish. I have left out a great deal. It was a sadly woven tapestry of long venal rants. Wishing to do right by George, my first thought was to chuck the lot, strangle it at birth. But he must be trying to say something, surely. I have put down what I think it was he wanted to say. Not all of it, but enough to convey his frustration, his rage, I hope.

Now all that remains is for me to round what happened next into as satisfactory a conclusion as may be fashioned.

BY WAY OF...

The next station is St Paul's.
Alight here for God,
Jingling tills and Gift Aid.
Alight here for the ghost of Diana
And the statue of Queen Anne,
Who is often mistaken
For Queen Victoria.

For some passengers, the down escalator never stops going down.

Sixty little feet, in a scuffed and battered variety of what passed for school shoes, trampled off the escalator. Under them, urgently and insistently nudging the combplate at its end, an old photograph. I made a mental note to clear it, or have it cleared once I had finished escorting the group down to the Eastbound Central Line platform. The children were returning to Leyton. It was already pushing half past two and the teacher leading the expedition became flustered, sighing, 'We've got a long way to go and a short time to get there.' I reassured her that there was a good service on the Central Line this afternoon and all the trains were running on time. When we arrived at the platform, I waited with the group. I had no clear view of exactly what happened next. It was all captured on CCTV.

Mind made up, George sidled through the motley gaggle of red sweat-topped children cluttering the platform, wending closer to the end where the train comes in. The class was dazed and tired after their trip to the British Museum, but still found the energy to chatter incessantly. What would be the point of waiting for them to go? They would only be followed by another school, and another, then the rush hour. George considered them for a moment. They appeared around seven or eight, and they were all colours of the rainbow. The more you looked, the more worn and sketchier their uniformity became. A girl had a green and yellow knitted cardigan, one of the boys wore a burgundy tracksuit bottom instead of school pants. Their clothes were faded, some with holes. At least one girl had on what looked like carpet slippers, while one lad's top was inside out and back to front. It seemed no single child wore matching socks; one girl had no socks at all. They were clustered in groups round Maypole parents or teachers, the whole array smelling of sweaty feet and school lunch.

Lennie the Faun's mistake had been to jump at the slow end of the platform. George composed himself and took a step back, the better to spring into the path of the oncoming train. To his left, the schoolchildren. The cheeky looking scruffy-haired blond boy closest him turned and flashed a dazzling smile. Without returning it, George grimly propelled himself forward. Glancing to his right, he caught sight of a young woman in a neat flower print blouse and well-tailored, blue trouser suit. She was tall, perhaps in her early twenties, with black shoulder length ringlets and a heavy fringe. A fair woman. It struck George as ironic that only now, so late, he should come to understand what 'fair' meant when said of a woman. He realised it was Linda! At that instant, mid jump, his nerve failed him. He panicked.

This was not the theatrically perfect leap George had hoped

for. He just flopped off the platform. Even as he toppled, he felt the falling void of poetry and hope. No, it was not the statement he intended. It also went a lot quicker, and slower, than he had imagined. But most of all, it went horribly wrong.

Linda gazed ahead, relaxedly surveying posters arched over the far side of the track, with cool blue eyes. Her job interview had gone splendidly; next year she would start as a trainee lawyer at Brennan Begley and Large. The dream was coming true. A long, happy career stretched ahead. That moment when Angela Large smiled and shook her hand, saying, 'Welcome aboard, Linda.' Pure gold. The relief; the pride. Now she would be working alongside David, her boyfriend. Life had never been more perfect.

Something moved, suddenly, to Linda's left. She turned and came face to face with George. Both goggled in shocked recognition. Linda realised, to her horror, that George had hold of her sleeve. Hair and fringe fluttered in the dry gusts that heralded the train's imminent arrival. He yanked her with him.

During that endlessness of falling, George and Linda shared a vision of the open-mouthed, wide-eyed terror that was the train driver's face. Warm blasts from the tunnel intensified. The train clattered into the station, brakes screeched, a whistle shrieked, but too late. Two figures spun off the platform.

George's attempt to steady himself, to stop, was too slow, too clumsy. Instead of stalling his fall, Linda had feebly resisted for the briefest of moments, before giving way. Worse yet, his heel caught on something. It was the little boy. The child teetered at the lip of the precipice, his smile now at odds with the fear in his eyes. He finally lost balance. The boy's face reddened, and he tumbled. In an instant, a quick-thinking mother grabbed his collar, holding him at an angle over the track in the path of the oncoming train, suspended as though he might lean that way forever. Her whole body shrouded in black, she swore loudly in Arabic, and with an almighty sigh, just in time, tugged him back to safety. He escaped the impact by a whisker. The woman let out a wail of relief, while the boy stared blankly, trembling, then threw his arms around her. They embraced; she pulled him closer, crying, thanking her God loudly. He buried his face in her robe, sobbing.

Was that Todd? Surely it was... there, behind fair Linda, George picked him out. He was standing confidently, holding his stick in the air with one hand, waving with the other, a wide, cheery smile gleaming white from his flawless, youthful, smooth-skinned face. 'Yes, George. I've been sent back until my task is done. Dinna wherry, I'll shepherd ye across, then I'll lead ye through the flowery maze!' He winked, grinning brightly. About his feet and the breadth of the platform, mice scurried helter-skelter among the people. They seemed to dance to the pulse, the rumble of the thundering train of death, their toes ever scampering. Today, the rustling railway ends here.

Instinctively, Linda clung to George, her satin cheek against his prickly, filthy stubble. The impact threw them apart; Linda rolled furthest from the wheels, looking straight into George's eyes as the train ran over his head. His puzzled expression did not change. For an age his features expanded, eyes filled with blood and bulged until the whole front of his head burst open, splattering over her. Linda watched her own outstretched hands go under a wheel. She felt nothing.

Children screamed. The words 'Gatwick, naturally' flashed in her mind as the underside of the cab clipped her head and unbearable noise gave way to silence. Deep, tranquil silence.

On the platform, distressed passengers stood, shocked. Bladders and bowels gave way. A man vomited. Yet the overwhelming sensation, even amid the noise and mayhem, was of stillness, as if, the pandemonium being too great, too sudden to comprehend, one blotted it out and mused upon the scene dispassionately from some other level. Chaos reigned briefly, until station staff put their familiar routine into motion.

'Ladies and gentlemen, due to an incident, passengers are advised to leave the Central Line platforms by the nearest exit, using all stairs and escalators.'

The calm voice jarred. Dazed people, some crying, were being shepherded from the platform. Overcoming her shock, the driver had already notified the Central Line controller and was now helping passengers off the train.

'The Central Line is suspended from Shepherd's Bush to Stratford due to a person under a train. Passengers are asked to use alternative routes. LRT buses and London Overground will be accepting tickets and Oyster cards on all reasonable alternative routes.'

Holborn station control room remained a phlegmatic oasis.

'That's the second this week, and it's only Wednesday!'

'It was George.'

'Who?'

'Old George, The Big Issue guy. It was him who went over.'

'Oh, no!'

'Yep. And he took someone with him.'

'Fuck, no? Fucking hell!'

'I was talking to him not an hour ago. I knew there was something up but I never expected anything like this.'

'Why? What did he say?'

'He said, 'How I feel and the way things are, are how I feel and the way things are.''

'Poor old sod. BTP are on scene now. The ambulance is on its way.'

'Who's working the platform?'

'Jerry. Tasneem's there, too. She went down with that group of children.'

'Oh good. Thank heavens it wasn't two rookies. They'll know what to do.'

Max Bygraves

The monitor let out a long plaintive bleep. Various coloured wavy lines on the screen fell flat. David gasped, bursting into great heaving sobs, reaching out. 'Linda! I... I... Nooooo!' A nurse gently pushed past him, took the wire that led from Linda's arm to the monitor and rammed the end in firmly. Within seconds the lines re-established their reassuring waviness.

It was three days before Linda regained consciousness. 'We weren't able to save your hands.

I'm sorry, there was nothing we could do.' Reeling, dark emptiness, for three more days...

KENSAL GREEN

The vendors built a shrine to George outside Pret. If they could, they would have dug up the pavement there and buried him with his things under a barrow, and around it, and the pavement companions of this beloved brother would have chanted their dirges. Instead, customers, friends, passers-by, and people who had seen it on the news or found out otherwise elaborated the grotto, hung tabards and blankets on it. They garlanded it with flowers, cuddly toys and scented candles that twinkled bright at the centre where George's own tabard hung, draped over his haversack. The wind fell still. The bones of dead umbrellas, as ever, adorned the pavement. Bees emerged from their energy drink bottle home into spring sunlight, and the little black bag of dogshit quivered with the restlessness of new life that would soon burst forth.

When the time came, and nobody had called for George's remains, they were interred without fanfare in a quiet corner of Kensal Green cemetery, along with two other unclaimed bodies, fished from the Thames.

Postscript

The day George jumped, one of the cleaners at Holborn found a photograph at the foot of an escalator. In it, young George was seated with a group of people. Beside him was another youth, with long, dark brown hair, playing a guitar.